CROSSING OVER EASY

Eastwind Witches 1

NOVA NELSON

ISBN: 978-0-9996050-5-9 (FFS Media)

Cover Design © FFS Media LLC

Cover design by Molly Burton at cozycoverdesigns.com

Crossing Over Easy, Eastwind Witches #1 / Nova Nelson -- 1st ed.

Previously published as *Crossing Over Easy: Witches of Salem, Nora Bradbury #1*

www.novanelson.com

CONTENTS

CROSSING OVER EASY

Eastwind Witches 1

NOVA NELSON

Chapter One

The windshield wipers swished frantically as a million raindrops darted through the beams of my LED headlights. I'd bought the new BMW M4 because it road tested well in conditions like this, but mostly because why not buy a BMW? I'd always wanted one, and I finally made enough money for it. It wasn't like I had any kids to spend my money on.

Or pets.

Or friends.

(Sad, I know.)

But not even my custom-upgrade headlights could make the long drive from New Orleans to Austin safe, even in dry conditions.

Going this slow on I-10 had to be illegal. Any second now, some dumb semi would come hauling tail behind me out of nowhere. The truck driver wouldn't expect a car to be creeping along at a leisurely 35 MPH, and then...

It would be the end of Nora Ashcroft. My life would find itself at a hasty, gruesome conclusion.

I wouldn't let that happen. I'd worked hard. Made something out of nothing. I'd put myself through culinary school, earned an MBA, opened one of Austin's hottest fine-dining experiences, and to top it all off, I'd paid off my student loan debt last month. Not only did I deserve to live, I deserved a freaking medal.

Although, when I considered it, it would be just my luck to die on this trip. Finally free from the shackles of debt, and *boom!* I'm painting the pavement.

I hope you'll excuse me if that seems a little doom and gloom. Behind the shiny veneer of business success, my life was nothing but doom and gloom. Or at least it was from the moment I got the devastating news about my parents, when I was only eleven, onward.

It was all about to change, though.

"Stupid, stupid, stupid," I berated myself. "I should've just stayed in New Orleans until tomorrow!"

But I knew I couldn't.

I'd gone to visit my sometimes man, Neil. He was my sometimes man for a few reasons. First, he lived eight hours away in New Orleans. I had the money to fly out there to see him every weekend if I wanted, except I was scared of flying.

Oh yes, *that* irrational fear.

I was one of those dummies who says, "I'm scared of a plane crash!" but will get in a car and drive for eight hours through darkness and pouring rain while truck drivers managing to keep one eye open, thanks to the miracles of meth, whiz past me at a cool 100 MPH.

Yeah, that's *so* much safer.

But fear rarely makes a whole heck of a lot of sense.

The second reason Neil was my sometimes man was that I could only tolerate him *sometimes.*

I wasn't that into Neil. He was rich, beautiful, ran with a crowd of other rich and beautiful people, but sometimes he would do or say things that made me wonder if he had a soul.

Then he'd give a million dollars to charity, and I'd usually forget about the previous indiscretion because people with souls didn't give that much to fight cancer or rebuild homes damaged by hurricanes, right?

But earlier that night, I'd reached the final straw. I was already a little on edge because of the voodoo woman we passed on Bourbon Street and what she'd said to me— I'll get to that, don't worry—so I just *couldn't* with him and his random outbursts of being a jerk. Plus, he did it to the one sort of person who I absolutely will not tolerate any mistreatment of: our server.

There is a special place in hell for people who mistreat the waitstaff at restaurants. I waited tables from the moment a little taqueria would let me when I was fourteen (okay, thirteen and a convincing liar) until the day I finally opened Chez Coeur five years previous, when I was twenty-seven. Fourteen years of it. Heck, there were even days when I'd pick up a few tables at Chez Coeur so I didn't lose touch with what the waitstaff was dealing with.

Plus, there was a slight thrill to waiting tables at my own restaurant. It felt like going undercover. No one ever guessed that the tall, fresh-faced, thirty-two-year-old woman was the owner (it's still quite the boys club, the restaurant industry). If a patron was rude to me, I would tell them to leave. If they asked for the manager, I would summon that night's the front-of-house manager. When the manager asked them to leave, the customer would ask to speak to the owner and *bam!* There I was, at their service.

The dumbfounded reactions I got from this were worth the mistreatment and then some. Once, a few of the nearby tables even applauded while I showed the rude, young couple to the door.

Neil was a trust-fund kid, though. Nothing against trust-funds—would've been nice if my parents had socked something away, though I guess no one *plans* to be murdered in their midthirties. But Neil had never worked a real job. He didn't understand what it was like to be on your feet all day in slip-proof shoes, your knees feeling like bone-on-bone, your lower back aching constantly. He'd never survived the futile pressure of having to please one stranger after another, to make everything right, no matter if it's your mistake or the customer is just having a bad day or they ordered something different than what they thought they'd ordered. Neil had never closed a restaurant at four in the morning, hurried home, flopped on his bed with his feet up on the headboard to give his swollen ankles and knees a break, then slept like the dead for three hours before waking up to open the next morning. He didn't know about working doubles. He didn't know about the creepy men who follow female servers to their cars. He didn't know that, yes, one customer might have ordered something simple and straightforward, but if that server has two other ten-tops sat in her section, a simple order is the easiest one to overlook.

And that was the exact situation that unfolded at our dinner that night. It was the server's mistake, sure, but she was clearly in the weeds with two massive parties where the guests were practically playing musical chairs. I watched the situation unfold from the calm of our two-top and already knew there was a good chance our order would take a while to come out. The poor girl could use a Xanax or thirty.

So when she brought over our entrees and forgot Neil's parmesan roasted brussels sprouts, I was actually impressed. I thought she'd have botched the order *much* worse than that.

Neil, however, was not impressed. He berated her. Asked her if his simple order was too much for her to remember. He suggested that next time she write it on a notepad. Better yet, work at a roadside diner where all the food looked the same and no one could tell if they got the wrong order.

The diner thing rubbed me wrong, but it also snapped me out of whatever persistent fugue state had kept me interested in him. I realized, even as the fragrance of foie gras filled my nostrils, that I couldn't be with someone who didn't appreciate the occasionally greasy diner food.

Not even as my sometimes man.

Neil, as it turned out, was the absolute worst.

And considering the voodoo woman had predicted my death in the next twenty-four hours (I didn't buy it, but it made for good motivation), I would be a total moron to spend my last remaining time on earth with this jerk.

I stood abruptly, my chair legs screeching on the

marble floors. Neil paused in his tirade, and both he and the waitress, Jenny (I learned her name because, you know, she's a human being), stared at me, their mouths little round o's.

"Neil. You're garbage at being a human," I said before I could stop myself. "To be honest, I'm starting to wonder if you're actually a sociopath. I must be incredibly lonely if I'm spending time around you." I grabbed my knee-length charcoal gray overcoat from the back of my chair and slipped it on over my white boat-neck tee and black trousers. "Oh, and before I forget, you're a *terrible* golfer."

I knew nothing about golf, but I knew that one would hit him where it hurt.

I pulled from my wallet whatever cash I had on me. Unfortunately, I'd decided on this grand gesture *before* realizing there were at least five hundred-dollar bills in the stack. But there was no balking now, not while Neil glared at me so disdainfully.

I held the cash out to our server. "Jenny, this is for you, because I know *he* won't tip well, and God knows you put up with enough at a place like this." I was losing my taste for fine dining with each passing second, which, as the owner of a fine-dining restaurant, was problematic for obvious reasons.

She took the money, and I left. I walked straight out of there feeling like a switch had been flipped, as if my priorities, long dormant, might have just reawakened.

It was a fresh start.

I didn't know how true and untrue that was.

A loud horn pulled me from my memories and I refocused my attention on the slick road. There were flashing lights up ahead. Blue and red. Cop lights. And some dimmer orange ones. What was going on?

I welcomed the excuse to slow down even more as I approached.

The wind began to blow sideways and sheets of rain danced across my headlights like apparitions in the night.

Apparitions. The voodoo woman had mentioned those. She said they'd been around me my whole life. Part of me knew that was true. I'd lived alone since my aunt, who'd taken me in when my parents were killed, had passed away herself fourteen years before. I'd never had a roommate, never had time for a pet (though I'd wanted one), but I'd always sensed the presence of something else around me. Maybe many something elses. There were nights when I swore I glimpsed something light and misty appear then fade in the corner of a room, or a dark figure pass across a doorway.

But I could never indulge those feelings, those inklings. I didn't have time for it, and besides, I lived alone. Accepting the idea that my condo might be haunted was too frightening to entertain. And work required as much attention as I could give it.

Oh yeah, and there was always the possibility that mental illness ran in my family. My aunt had hinted at as much. (She wasn't a pleasant woman, so I can't say I was especially torn up when she died.)

When your options are either that you see ghosts or possess a hereditary mental illness, you tend to want to opt out of the choice altogether.

What can I say? Denial has always been one of my strengths.

By the looks of the barricade, I-10 was closed and

rerouted north for a while. I'd passed the sign for Beaumont just a few minutes before, so at least I had *some* idea of where I was.

But whose genius idea was it to reroute a major highway?

Well, I suppose it was the middle of the freaking night. Not exactly peak traffic hours. If it had to be done, the time was ripe.

The orange detour signs were hardly visible in the torrent, so I turned north and gave my phone the voice command to "take me home."

"*Okay,*" replied my most loyal friend. (Sad but true.) "*I am taking you home. You will arrive at home by seven forty-two a.m.*"

"Thanks, Google," I said before realizing I'd just thanked an electronic device.

I seriously considered following up with, "Okay, Google, how do I make friends?" but didn't want to embarrass myself in front of the technology.

I took it slow along the farm-to-market road. I'd show that voodoo woman who was boss. I would *not* be "joining the spirits before sunrise," like she'd said. Not driving twenty-five miles an hour, I wouldn't. I could run straight into a tree and not even have whiplash at this speed. And besides, my expensive new car would never let that happen. It had more sophisticated accident avoidance mechanisms than I could count, to the point where it seemed engineered specifically for drunk drivers.

The car was idiot proof. I'd once spilled a hot latte on my lap and accidentally yanked the steering wheel to the left ... except the car didn't allow that. It beeped ferociously at me and the steering wheel didn't budge an inch. Afterward, I was thankful, but also fully creeped out. *I can't let you do that, Nora*, I'd imagined it saying in the voice of HAL from 2001: *A Space Odyssey*.

I passed a sign notifying me that I was now entering into Eastwind, Texas.

I'd spent my life in the Lone Star State, yet I'd never heard of this place. Where was I?

I snuck a quick glance at my phone, but the screen was dark. Shoot. I pressed the button to wake it up, but nothing.

"Okay, Google."

No response. No cute beep to let me know it was listening, awaiting orders like a good little phone servant.

I turned my eyes back to the road, and shouted, "Okay, Google, quit playing. I don't know where I am."

Still nothing.

Crap. This wasn't happening. How was I supposed to get home without my phone? I couldn't stop at a gas station and ask for directions because it was the middle of the night, and this was not the type of town that had a gas station. Maybe an old-timey filling station with an attendant who'd served a little time but had a heart of gold. But no gas station. No Shells, no Exxons, no Chevrons.

Adrenaline got the best of me, and my lead foot acted up.

I may not have known where I was going, but I was going to get there quick. Ain't nobody got time for being lost. Especially me. I had a meeting with an investor the following evening, someone who wanted to open a Chez Coeur in Dallas. I had places to be, and I wasn't looking to wind up in some *Deliverance* scenario out here in the boonies.

As my pulse increased, so did my speed. I realized there were no other cars within sight. What had happened to all the highway traffic? Shoot, did I miss a turn in the detour? I must have.

The next split second dragged out for an eternity.

The dark figure in the road.

My headlights piercing right through it.

My dash lights going black.

My startled yell as I yanked the steering wheel hard to the right to avoid hitting whatever was in the road.

The jolt of the front tires over the dirt shoulder.

The *complete absence* of all the safety features I paid a fortune for!

My headlights shutting off.

At the very last moment, the sight of the thick tree trunk in the moonlight on a collision course for the front of my car.

And then the bone-crushing impact.

And then nothing.

Chapter Two

Someone was giving my face a sponge bath.

No, wait. Was someone making out with me?

Yeah, that seemed more accurate.

They weren't great at it, though. Sloppy technique.

I opened my eyes but couldn't make sense of my surroundings right away.

Something big and fluffy hovered over me, but the only detail I could make out against the dark canopy of trees was the pink tongue.

"Stop it. I'm not that kinda girl," I muttered through my haze.

It wasn't *entirely* true. I'd kissed a few guys whose names I didn't know (work hard, play hard), but none of them had ever been this hairy.

I pushed the thing off of me, and only after getting some distance did I realize what it was: a giant black dog. Actually, *was* that even a dog? I'd never seen a dog that big. It was the size of a pony, easily.

The animal backed off a few steps and stared at me

with droopy yellow eyes as I propped myself up on my elbows. "Yuck," I said, wiping the slobber from my face. "Thanks but no thanks."

"Well, excuse me for helping," replied the hound before he turned and trotted off into the darkness.

But no, that couldn't be right. Dogs didn't talk.

Hmm ... Put a tally mark in the "mental illness" column.

Or maybe I'd just hit my head. Where was I? What had happened? How did I get here?

It started to come back to me—the detour, the black figure in the middle of the road ... the tree.

But when I looked around, it didn't add up. Where was my car? Where was the road?

All around me were tall trees stretching up toward a dark, starry sky I glimpsed through the canopy. I lay on soft pine needles in a tiny clearing.

East Texas had tall trees, but not like this. This place reminded me more of the Pacific Northwest, another place I'd wanted to visit but always lacked either the time or funds to do so.

Were it light outside, the woods might've been lovely and magical and inviting. For some reason, though, I suspected they would still be eerie in the daytime.

But in the dead of night, I was absolutely certain that they were downright creepy. I needed to get out of here, to a town.

I stood cautiously, worrying that the accident might have left me with some injuries that had yet to register with my rattled brain, but that didn't seem to be the case. I felt fine. Great, actually.

Well, except for the totally disoriented in the middle of nowhere part.

Dusting the pine needles off my overcoat, I looked down at my white shirt and black trousers to check for tears. Other than the dried leaves and needles clinging to them, they looked fine. No stains, no rips. What a strange bit of good luck.

I headed in the direction of the black dog, thinking he was probably more familiar with this landscape and wouldn't head straight off a cliff or toward a bear cave or whatever else might be lurking out here. If he was like all the dogs I'd encountered in my life, he was probably following his nose to food.

My stomach growled. Because I'd split before the main course, the last thing I'd eaten was a few mussels as an appetizer at my dinner with Neil. And before that was a light breakfast: one slice of fresh-baked bread with a locally grown and canned apricot pear jam spread over the top. It was delicious, sure, but what I craved now was a greasy burger or ten. Fine dining could be fun, but I was far too hungry for the minuscule portion size.

After ten minutes of walking, the first glimmer of light poked between tree trunks. I sped up.

Then there were more lights.

And more.

I jogged the last hundred yards until I broke from the forest and found myself on the edge of a tiny town.

Lamps lit a narrow street stretching out straight ahead of me, bordered on either side by a spattering of shops whose signs I couldn't make out from this angle and in such low light. But up ahead, where the road teed, was the most beautiful thing I'd ever laid eyes on.

The lights were on inside, and an *open* sign glowed on and off. The dang thing might as well have been flashing, *There is a God!* for how much hope it gave me.

The metal exterior glistened in the moonlight as I approached. Long windows spanned the length of the building, allowing the full glory of the diner to be visible to a hungry traveler such as myself. Patrons filled most of the booths along the front windows, and behind them, a long countertop spread out.

Memories of my parents began to surface. I didn't have many left, but I held on tight to what few remained. The ones that visited me now were of the Sundays we spent together. They took me to this little rundown diner that had been an Austin staple for decades and was one of the last holdouts against the chain restaurants and places like ... well, like Chez Coeur. We went every week, and the wait staff knew my name, treated me like a surrogate daughter. I had free rein of the place and no one objected. Julio, the manager, even let me go back in the kitchen once (a total health-code no-no) and showed me how to make his famous migas.

And then someone went and murdered my parents, and in doing so, also stole the family I had at Rupert's All-Night Diner.

I hadn't thought about those Sundays in years, but the delicious scent of beef patties and french fries issuing from up ahead triggered the memories in an avalanche.

Above the front door glowed a neon sign reading *Medium Rare*. The letters flashed in sequence, one at a time, then all together.

"Listen, diner, you had me at 'open.' No need to try so hard," I mumbled as I passed underneath the showy sign and entered an olfactory trip down memory lane. I shut my eyes and inhaled deeply. If someone could distill this smell into a liquid, I would bathe in it.

Oh, wait. That would just be griddle grease. Okay, never mind about the bathing part. Let the record show I would not bathe in griddle grease.

"Have a seat anywhere!" hollered a voice from behind the long counter. I opened my eyes to see a bulky middle-aged man with a kind face and thick, hairy forearms wave to me before disappearing between the metal double doors into the kitchen.

"Thanks," I hollered back, but I don't know if he heard me over the noise from the other diners and the loud sizzling of meat on the grill.

I looked around for an open booth, and that's when I discovered that, okay, something was a little off.

I do this. When I get freaked out beyond words, I resort to understatement. It's part of the not letting people know you're afraid thing, which is rule number one to being a single, independent, female business owner in an industry run by egomaniacal men.

So when I say something was a little off, what I mean was I saw the Grim Reaper.

The freaking Grim Reaper. He was sitting alone in a booth at the back of the diner, all decked out in his hood, his sickle leaning against the window as he shoved his mouth full of a cheeseburger.

When he noticed me looking, he nodded casually and waved hello.

Noooooope. Not waving back.

I did a one-eighty and headed in the other direction

down the row of booths toward an empty one at the opposite end from Death.

Everyone stared at me.

They must not get many new people in town, I thought.

I smiled at them as I passed, trying to make a good first impression and act like I wasn't totally losing it over the Grim Reaper's presence.

Then I spotted the legs on one family. They dangled underneath the tabletop and were only visible for a moment as I walked past, but they were clearly goat legs. All of them had goat legs. My eyes darted up to their faces, which followed me like sunflowers follow the sun. Horns. They also had horns. I'd almost missed the things poking out beneath each person's curly hair, but sure as anything, there they were.

As much as I wanted to do a double take, it seemed rude, and I was pretty sure it would yield the same results. I did, however, glance over at them once I sat down, because, who knows, it could have been a family of goats sitting in that booth, and I'd just been confused and thought their top half was human.

But nope. Two mostly human parents, one mostly human daughter, and one mostly human son. All with horns.

It was fine, though. I wasn't totally losing my mind.

I'm not totally losing my mind. I'm not totally losing my mind. I'm not totally losing my mind. I repeated that a few more times in my head. You know, like a sane person does.

Had the smell of steak and eggs not been so potent, I would have high-tailed it out of Medium Rare and never looked back (except maybe to make sure the Grim Reaper wasn't following me).

I was in a tight spot, but that was okay. I'd been on my own for long enough and from such a young age that the only thing I was better at than getting myself into a tight spot was getting myself out of one. I would sit here, not show fear, and order myself some food.

Except …

My wallet was in the car. Dang. Could I dine and dash?

No, I couldn't afford such bad karma when Death was checking me out from across the room.

I'd just explain it to the nice hairy-armed man when he came over and took my order. I'd say I was lost, didn't have my wallet on me—maybe I'd even mention the car accident for pity points—and then I'd offer to help with dishes in the kitchen in return for a meal.

With a plan in place, I allowed myself a deep breath.

But the plan fell apart immediately when *he* approached my table.

Whoa.

He was beautiful. I know men prefer "handsome" or "sexy," but neither seemed quite accurate for him. He was tall, strong but not in that awful "yeah, I lift" sort of way. More like the way men get from actually *doing* productive things like farming or logging or inviting a lost, tired stranger back to his place to—

"Hey there," he said, a big, goofy grin lighting up his already glowing complexion. His hair was the color of wet sand, short in an unmanaged sort of way, and he had the beginning of a beard and mustache growing in. I was familiar with that sort of facial hair. It signaled that he'd shaved early in the morning before a long day. People talk about five o'clock shadow, but in the service industry, we see three o'clock shadow. As in three in the morning. He'd probably worked a double shift, yet here he was, smiling like there was nowhere he'd rather be.

"Hi," I said.

"You're new." Not a question.

"Yes."

He wiped a hand on his apron and offered it to me. "I'm Tanner."

Talk about service with a smile. I took a mental note of how surprisingly pleasant it was to have a proper introduction with my server—maybe I'd institute the policy at Chez Coeur when I got back.

But no, the patrons at my restaurant didn't want to connect with the waitstaff; they wanted to distance themselves.

"Nora," I said, shaking his hand.

He had a firm grip, but so did I.

He nodded, impressed, and flashed me a half-grin before asking, "When'd you cross over?"

"Excuse me?" I spat, my eyes flickering over to Death, who was leaning his elbows on the table as he stared dreamily out of the window.

"I just mean, when'd you get into Eastwind?"

"Is that still where I am?" I asked.

He narrowed his eyes, studying me. "Huh. Wow. You don't know where you are. That must be alarming." Then, to my surprise, he slid into the booth across from me. Rubbing his hands together, he said, "Okay. This means I'm your first point of contact." He shook out his hands at the wrists and took a deep breath. "Phew! I've heard about people being the first point of contact for newcomers, but I never thought I'd get the chance."

What in the heck was he talking about? I knew rural Texas could be a bore fest, but surely they had to get people passing through every now and again.

"Ask me a question," he said. "Anything."

I easily settled on one. "Is that the Grim Reaper over there, or have I lost my mind?"

He tossed a glance over his shoulder. "I don't know about *the* grim reaper, but yeah, he's *a* grim reaper." Leaning forward, he added, "He prefers if you just call him Ted."

"Ted?" I echoed dumbly.

"Yeah," he said. "And I mean, I guess it makes sense. I wouldn't want people just calling me 'witch,' you know?"

"Why would people call you witch?"

Tanner scrunched up his nose and turned his head slightly to the side. Did he think I was just messing with him? Was the answer that obvious?

"Because I'm a witch," he said.

Okay, so the answer *was* obvious, if given the necessary information, which I hadn't had. But now I did.

"You're a witch?" I asked.

He nodded.

"Is that what they call you? A witch? Not a wizard or a warlock?"

It wasn't the most productive line of questioning on my part. Instead, I should've asked, "Are you screwing with me?" because witches aren't a thing.

Except I'd just had it validated that the Grim Reaper —I'm sorry, *Ted*—was less than twenty yards away from me, and, if my eyes were to be believed, there was a family of goat people three booths down. So, sure, why couldn't this gorgeous man be a witch?

I guess my question had offended him, though. He sat up straight, raising his chin. "Witches can be dudes."

I held up my hands defensively. "Sorry, sorry. Didn't mean to offend you."

His strong shoulders softened. "Nah, don't worry about it. Being a witch is awesome enough that I don't mind the occasional diss from people about male witches. But you'll figure out the perks soon enough, I guess."

His grin was so warm, it sucked me in and I almost didn't notice what he was implying. "Hold up. Why would I figure out the perks?"

He wobbled his head side to side anxiously. "Well, because, you know, the odds are … you're a witch."

I laughed. "Okay, you got me." I looked around the restaurant. "Where are the hidden cameras?"

"Hidden what?" he asked, sounding concerned.

"Cameras." I waved it off. "Never mind. I'm just saying you have to be kidding me, right? Why on earth would you think I was a witch?"

He paused, worrying his lip. "Well," he said, "because you're not a leprechaun or a faun or a vampire— I can tell that by looking at you. There are a few other things that can be ruled out just by looking at you, but I won't bore you with all that. Mostly, I'm thinking you're a witch because, outside of the occasional Avalonian who visits, which, no offense, I can tell you're definitely *not* just by how you're dressed, the only new people we get in Eastwind are witches."

It was a lot to process. I decided to chip away at it one small piece at a time. "Now, I have a lot of questions about what you just said, but I'm gonna put a pin in them, because there's a burning question I can't shake."

"Go ahead."

I leaned forward, whispering, "Does that family over there have goat legs?"

His hazel eyes lightened and he laughed. It sounded like spring felt. "You mean the Tomlinsons?"

I shrugged. Sure, the Tomlinsons. As if I would've introduced myself to them already, said, "Hi, I'm Nora Ashcroft. And you are?" and then casually walked away like they didn't all have hooves.

"They're fauns," he continued. "They don't have those where you're from?"

"Nope."

"So what *do* they have where you're from?"

"Just plain humans."

He scrunched up his nose, shaking his head vaguely. "I don't understand. What do you mean, plain?"

"Like me. Just a person. I don't know."

He whistled low. "Sounds like a boring place, no offense. Bet you're glad you wound up here."

I chuckled. "Reserving judgment."

He slid out of the booth. "Now I got a question for you, Nora. What can I get you started for breakfast?"

Chapter Three

Watching the way Tanner related to everyone in Medium Rare made me hope that if I ever got out of this town, he would come with me. Chez Coeur could use someone like him. He just had this way about him that lit a lamp behind the other person's eyes. There was an instant connection when he slid into my booth and acted like I was the only thing in the entire world that mattered in that moment.

I shamelessly scoped him out as he brought a slice of pie over to Ted at the far end of the restaurant, and even Death himself seemed to light up when Tanner looked at him.

And I have to say, I was wildly impressed by Tanner's ability to remain so casual and friendly with Death.

I could have sat there all night watching Tanner work his magic, trying to figure out what his secret was, except my stomach was straight up eating itself.

While the front-of-house service was great, the back-of-house could use a little help. Had it just *felt* like I was sitting there for half an hour, or had it actually been that long?

The delay allowed my mind to run laps over the events of the night. Boy, had it been a long one.

I was jonesing something fierce for my cell phone. I needed to get in touch with Georgina, the manager in charge of opening Chez Coeur the next day, to let her know I wouldn't be in. We had a huge delivery of duck arriving first thing, and I was always the one that handled those deliveries since there was usually an inventory discrepancy and ...

Man, my life back home was tedious. Ted and the Tomlinsons (great TV show title, by the way) were vastly more interesting than anything I'd seen or done in the past ... forever?

No, I wasn't going to sit here and trash my whole life. I'd worked hard for that life. I'd worked my butt off for it seventy hours a week for years.

Where was my food?

Impatient, I looked around for Tanner to see if he'd check on it for me, but I couldn't spot him. Maybe he was already in the back checking on it.

That was fine. I knew my way around a restaurant.

Abandoning my booth, I pushed my way through the double doors separating the front-of-house from the back.

The sound of grease on a hot griddle was deafeningly loud, the kitchen swelteringly hot. I peeked around the corner toward the line, looking for someone to bug. But there was nobody manning the griddle. Or anything. Where *was* everyone?

A loud thud me caused me to jump, and I froze for a second, looking around. A door slammed and then there was silence. Something wasn't right. I knew it instantly, could feel the presence of it in my bones. But I steadied myself and followed the source of the sound to the manager's office where ...

"Oh no." Facedown on the floor was the man who'd greeted me when I'd first entered Medium Rare. His hairy arms were spread out to either side of him, and he wasn't moving. I'm no doctor, but I was pretty sure that red stuff bubbling from a gash on the back of his head was blood.

My mind only noticed the frying pan on the floor next to him in passing as I bent down, yelling, "Sir? Sir? Can you hear me? Are you alright, sir?"

No response.

For whatever reason, I didn't want to touch him. Maybe it was the intimacy of the moment. We were two strangers thrust together into this horrible situation, and now I had to take this relationship to the next level by touching him?

I got over myself and grabbed his thick forearm, shaking it gently. "Sir? Can you—"

"What is going— Oh no."

It was Tanner. I didn't have to turn around to know it was him. His voice was already stored firmly in my memory.

"Bruce!" he yelled, shaking the man much harder than I had. "Bruce, you okay, buddy?"

"I don't think he is," I mumbled.

Tanner glared at me then reached forward and put two fingers on Bruce's neck. He paused. Grunting slightly, he readjusted the placement of his fingers and then waited again. Still nothing.

He rolled back on his heels until his butt hit the cold tile floor of the manager's office, then he put his head in his hands.

I didn't know what to do. Leaning over, I placed a comforting hand on his shoulders, but he shrugged it off and stood abruptly. "You did this?"

I jumped up too. "No! Of course not!"

"Then why were you back here?"

"My food was taking forever and you weren't around so— Hey, wait! Where were *you*?"

He cringed. "I had to use the restroom. Can't a guy use the restroom at some point in his double?"

We stared at each other for only a second more before I was sure he was telling the truth. He must have sensed as much from me because we both turned back toward the body.

"What now?" I asked.

He ran a hand down his face. "I guess we send an owl to Deputy Manchester."

"Are you joking?"

He was not.

Sending an owl is exactly what it sounds like. Tanner grabbed a pen and slip of paper from Bruce's desk and scribbled on it before telling me to follow him, explaining, "No offense, but I don't think either of us should be alone with the body until Manchester arrives. Could look suspicious."

I agreed and stepped with him out the back door and into the cold night air. To the right of the door was a brass bell attached to the wall. Tanner rang it and a moment later, an owl appeared out of the dark sky and landed on a brass perch just below the bell. Once Tanner had attached the message, he said, "Deputy Stu Manchester" and the owl was off.

* * *

Deputy Stu Manchester arrived no more than fifteen minutes later, and his presence freed up Tanner to clear out the restaurant, telling everyone their meal was free and if they hadn't gotten their meal yet, they could come back next time and get a free one on him.

Once the deputy had covered the body, he pulled the two of us outside for questioning, though he made whoever he wasn't speaking with sit out of earshot in case we were trying to "get our stories straight."

I had the impression that Deputy Manchester lived for this type of action. Not Bruce's death specifically, but murders. He was like a kid in a candy shop and did a poor job of remaining nonchalant in the face of something as interesting as this. I supposed it made sense; a tiny town in Texas (though I was starting to think I wasn't in Texas anymore) wouldn't have a lot going on. His days were probably spent on calls about kids trespassing and stolen livestock.

He held a notepad at chest level as he inspected me. "Ashcroft, eh? Never met an Ashcroft before. You make that name up?"

I sighed. "Uh, no. I'm sorry, but is my name relevant?"

"You never know what's relevant to a murder case, Ms. Ashcroft. It *is* miss and not missus, right?" Was he coming on to me? My eyes danced over to Tanner, where he leaned against a tree twenty yards off.

"Miss is fine."

He scratched out something on his notepad and then tucked it into his breast pocket. "Ms. Ashcroft—"

"Just Nora is fine."

"Okay then. Nora, I'd like you to look at this from my perspective. A well-established business owner is murdered out of the blue, and when I take a good look at the situation, the only new element I can find in this equation is you. What do you say to that?"

I shrugged. "Look harder?" I knew I shouldn't sass him, but I was hungry, tired, and being accused of murder in so many words. That didn't exactly bring out the best in me.

He puffed up his chest. "Of course I'll keep looking at things. Listen, missy—"

"Nora."

"—I've been doing this job a long time. I don't need your help on it!"

"So then we're done with questions? Great. I'm starving."

He grunted. "We're not done with ... Well, no, I guess we are. I asked you all my questions. Okay. I better call in Ted to clean this place up. Don't go leaving town! I might have more questions for you once I inspect the scene further."

"Of course." I decided not to mention that the main reason I agreed was that I currently had no viable option for leaving town. Not until I could solve the mystery of the disappearing BMW.

Deputy Manchester turned and stomped into the diner.

The bright moon lit the dark sky and a chilly wind

rushed through. I wrapped my arms around myself and shivered before he placed a warm hand between my shoulder blades. "Don't let him get to you," Tanner said, rubbing my back slowly. "He's a good guy, but he gets a little excited when anything interesting happens."

"You know him well?" I asked. The lamplight glimmered in his hazel eyes.

"I don't know about that. But we've had our fair share of ... exchanges."

Whoa. "You have run-ins with the law a lot?" Did Tanner have a bad-boy side? Who would've thought?

He grimaced slightly. "Ehh, I wouldn't say that exactly. It's a long story. Let's just say every time someone ends up dead in Eastwind, I find myself somehow a suspect."

"Do people end up dead here a lot?"

Meeting my gaze, he sighed. "Too often. Guess that's what comes of a bunch of dangerous creatures all gathered into a small town."

"Geez, you're really selling me on the place." But I found that I was starting to accept the idea that I might not be crazy and Tanner might not be lying, and there *could* exist a town full of creatures I always thought dwelled solely in fairy tales and myths. Believing such a thing almost felt natural ... once I got past everything I'd ever learned about the world.

Tanner chuckled. "If we're going to be here a while, we might as well go inside where it's warm."

No argument there.

Once we were in the diner, I parked it on a tall stool and he stood on the other side of the counter. "Do you like pie?" he asked, leaning forward on his elbows.

"What kind of a monster doesn't?" As soon as I'd said it, it occurred to me that "monster" might be some kind of slur in a town like this. I cringed, but he didn't seem offended.

Grinning, he pointed at me and winked. "You're my kinda gal."

He didn't mean it like *that*, right?

Two pies were on display at the end of the counter. He removed the glass domes and plated two pieces, one of each pie. Setting the plate between us and two forks next to it, he said, "Cherry and blueberry. You pick your favorite, and I'll eat the other."

"What if I want both?" I asked. Sadly enough, this was my attempt at flirting. I admit it was not the best approach. But I was exhausted and starving, so gluttony was about the sexiest thing I could think of just then.

Anyway, it achieved its intended effect. His head jerked back and a delicious half-grin appeared on his face. "Dang! *Definitely* a girl after my own heart!"

I thought about laughing and saying, "I'm only kidding, one piece is enough," except that would've been a lie. I couldn't remember the last time I'd indulged in good old-fashioned pie. All the desserts I'd eaten lately were "delicate" with "subtle hints" of this spice or that random root found only in the Amazon Rainforest.

But gosh dangit! I wanted *pie*! Real pie! Pie made with butter and flour and canned berries and sugar. Mostly sugar. I wanted to stuff my face with it. So no, I didn't tell him I was kidding about eating both pieces because I absolutely wasn't. The end was nigh for these two slices, and it might take Deputy Manchester handcuffing me to the barstool for the rest of the pies to avoid the same fate.

And, oh holy smokes, was the blueberry delicious. And the cherry. I'm not embarrassed to say I made quick work of both. "Tanner, did you make these?"

He grinned modestly. "Yeah. Baking pies is kind of my thing."

"You have to teach me how to make these."

He eyed me skeptically. "You planning on sticking around long enough for me to teach you how to make my famous pies?"

Oh, right. I wasn't planning on sticking around. Not even for Tanner. Not even for *pie*.

Before I could come up with something smart to say, the bell above the front door tinkled, capturing my attention. I turned to see who had entered and nearly jumped out of my skin.

The thing is, no matter how many encounters you have with Death, it's always a shock when he shows up.

"Hey, Ted," Tanner said casually as the grim reaper approached the bar.

"Hello again, Tanner!" Ted replied. His voice was a deep death rattle, like someone shaking a bag of old bones at the bottom of a well. "It's so crazy, right?" Ted chuckled, sending chills up my spine. "I was just in here, and then Bruce was killed, and I totally had nothing to do with it, you know?"

Tanner nodded kindly.

Ted shook his head and grinned. "It's just so random. What a coincidence. I had nothing to do with it, by the way. So, uh ... if anyone asks, would you just let them know?" He glanced at me and his eyes were two endless pits. "People here tend to assume I bring death with me wherever I go. Totally not the case. Do I have crazy timing? Yes, I'll admit that. But it's not like I'm an omen or anything. Heh-heh."

"Uh-huh," I said as cheerily as possible. The last thing I wanted to do was put Ted on the defensive.

He turned to Tanner. "By the way, I was thinking of getting a game of bridge together on Saturday." Ted pointed a finger gun at him. "You in?"

Tanner nodded noncommittally. "Let me look at me schedule, Ted, and I'll get back to you. You should, um, probably ..." He hitched a thumb over his shoulder toward the back, where Bruce's body was still lying lifeless on the floor, staining the tile with blood.

"Oh! Right!" Ted laughed and leaned playfully toward me, bringing a gloved hand up to his mouth to stage whisper to me, "The old nine to five. Gotta pay the bills though, right?"

"Heh. Yeah," I said, counting down the seconds until I could have a little more space between us.

He nodded at Tanner. "I like her. Just something about her. I don't know. You should hang on to this one."

"Oh, no," Tanner stammered awkwardly, "we're not ... she's not my ... we just found the crime scene together."

"Okay," he said, unconvinced. "Sure. Just saying, if you don't, *someone* might snatch her up." He winked at Tanner. "Either way,"—he turned to me—"you should come along with him to bridge night." He leaned his sickle back against his shoulder. "Alright. I'll get to it. Catch ya later!"

I don't *think* the last bit was intended as a threat.

As soon as he was out of sight, I turned to Tanner. "Are you going to bridge night?"

"Not a chance."

When I started laughing, so did he, and the last bit of my energy evaporated. I sighed. "It's been a really long night."

He dragged his fingers through his hair. "Yeah. Sure has." He paused, staring down at the countertop. "I can't believe Bruce is dead. It's just ... it's strange."

"Were you two close?"

"Yeah, for the most part. Something changed in him recently, though. He seemed just a little disconnected, and twice I caught him talking to himself in the storage closet. No, not talking to himself," he corrected, "talking to someone else. Maybe a few other people. But no one was there." He shook his head to clear it. "Then sometimes he would be just fine. Like tonight. He seemed a little like his old self tonight. Our cook called in sick, and Bruce said he'd fill in. He got his start way back when as a line cook. Jumped in whenever he could. Still loved it."

"I'm sorry," I said. What else was there to say? Bruce's death was settling in for Tanner, and it wasn't hard for me to tap into memories of what it felt like when the shock wore off and the grim news filled its place.

"I was worried about his health, what with the talking to himself and acting anxious most of the time," Tanner continued. "Turns out, his health wasn't a problem. A frying pan was." He grimaced and turned his attention to me. "You must be exhausted. You got somewhere to stay tonight?"

"I figured I'd go look for my car, take a cat nap in it, and then get on the road again."

He nodded slowly. From his expression, it looked like he was starting to doubt my sanity as much as he had Bruce's. "Well, I don't know what a car is, but can I make a suggestion?"

Maybe I *was* going crazy, because I could have sworn he'd just said he didn't know what a car was. "Uh, sure."

"Stay in town tonight. If you try to take off, it's going to look a little suspicious, don't you think?"

He had a point. Plus, Deputy Manchester had instructed me to stick around. "Okay. But I don't know anyone in town except you, I guess."

Then it occurred to me where this conversation was likely heading.

Oh. My. God. Was this gorgeous man about to invite me back to his place for the night? I might've been bone tired, but I wasn't too tired to b—

Eh-hem, what I mean to say is I could've rallied if the night called for it.

He pressed his lips together, nodding, deep thoughts swirling behind his beautiful exterior. "You know what? Ruby True." He waggled a finger at me. "Yeah, I bet she would let you use her spare bedroom upstairs. She usually charges for it, but I bet I can sweet-talk her into giving you a free night, considering the circumstances."

"And who is Ruby?" What I'd wanted to ask was "What is Ruby?" but that seemed impolite. Still, I wasn't looking to spend the night at a dragon's house or whatever. Did they have dragons here?

"She's an old woman."

Well, wasn't this a delightful twist. I'd hoped I'd be

spending an evening with Mr. Sexy Witch, but instead, I would get to spend a night in some dusty grandma's attic, fighting off moths, no doubt.

Still, better than a dragon, I supposed. "Oh. Sounds exciting."

"It usually is with her." There was no sarcasm in his statement. "I'll send an owl and ask the fearsome Deputy Stu if we're free to leave." He flashed me a quick grin, leaving me a little lightheaded (or was that the carb rush after devouring two pieces of pie on an empty stomach?), and disappeared into the back.

I sighed. It looked like I'd be spending the night in Eastwind.

Okay, I could handle that. What was the worst that could happen in a town filled with deadly supernatural creatures?

Chapter Four

"We're good to go," Tanner said, emerging from the back room again, a heavy jacket slung over his shoulder. "Sent an owl to Ruby, so she'll be expecting us."

"Us?"

"Yeah, of course. Unless ... you know how to get to Ruby's house?"

"Ah, right."

He held out his jacket. "Here. It's a little bit of a walk."

"I already have an overcoat," I said, holding my arms out to show him.

"I'm not in-the-know about fashion," he said, eyeing my coat suspiciously, "but that strikes me as more of an accessory than an actual coat."

I shrugged a shoulder. It'd been plenty earlier tonight, when I'd left New Orleans. But the temperature *had* dropped significantly since then.

"Yeah, okay. You're right." Tanner was half a foot taller than me, probably a few inches north of six feet.

That, coupled with the heavy circumference of his biceps, meant his jacket easily slid on above my overcoat without bunching. I pulled it tight around me. "Thanks." His scent wafted from the jacket into my nostrils. There was something earthy about it, almost like a mixture of rosemary and sage. And cherry pie.

"Nobody you'd want to spend the night with lives in the Outskirts," he explained as we emerged into the cold air and strolled down the dirt road toward, I presumed, the center of town. "But it's a perfect place for Medium Rare. Mostly werewolves live out here, and boy do they love their steak and eggs."

"You just said 'werewolves' right?"

He chuckled. "Yep."

"Okay, just checking."

"I take it they don't have those where you're from."

"Not that I know of."

We must have passed a hundred street lamps before I realized they weren't electric. Just old-fashioned gas lamps, by the looks of them. That relaxed me for some reason.

The dirt streets transitioned to cobblestone a block further on, and buildings became less sparse. "Bruce could have afforded a place closer into town, but he wanted to be where his kind were located. Werewolves have to put on airs in Eastwind proper, but not in the Outskirts."

"Bruce was a werewolf?" I asked. My mind traveled to his hairy forearms. But no, I'd met plenty of men with hairy forearms who *weren't* werewolves.

Or so I thought. Who even knew anymore?

"Yep. But he wasn't like a lot of them. Werewolves

can be kind of ..." Tanner looked around to make sure the coast was clear, then he leaned toward me. "They can be a little unruly." He straightened up. "But not Bruce. Well, except when it came to Jane. Doesn't matter. I don't want to speak ill of the dead. Bruce was a great guy. Man, it feels weird to talk about him in the past tense." He shook his head. "He was just so ... what's the word? Vivacious. Yeah, I think that's it. He was loud, friendly, joked around with everyone. Heck, even the name of the diner is a long-standing joke."

"Medium Rare?"

He nodded.

"I guess I don't get it."

"Yeah, he had to explain it to me, too. It's a werewolf thing. They always want their steaks rare, but they're embarrassed to admit it. It reminds the rest of us that they're always a few seconds away from becoming a wild animal. Lots of witches don't like that. I don't care one way or another. Besides, we all have the ability to be good or bad, no matter what we are.

"Anyway, when werewolves order their meat rare, they get judgmental looks, I guess. So they always ask for their steaks to be cooked medium rare. It's sort of an inside joke. Bruce told me about it, though, so that I knew to write 'rare' on the order whenever werewolves ordered it medium rare. The name also lets the werewolves around Eastwind know that they're always welcome in Bruce's establishment ... so long as they didn't stir up trouble."

"That makes sense," I said, feeling a little overwhelmed by the reality that werewolf subculture was now a thing I needed to be socially conscious of.

When Tanner stopped short and put his arm out in front of me, I dug my heels in, too. He looked around, his eyes wide. "Something's coming," he said.

Chills ran down my spine and I couldn't breathe until a dark figure emerged from the shadows. For a moment, I thought of the figures that had stepped into the road, causing the car crash that had landed me in this strange situation. But when the figure stepped into the lamplight, I realized I didn't need to worry.

"You again," said the giant black dog. *"Just my luck."*

"Whoa," Tanner said, taking a step back. "Careful, Nora. Could be a hellhound. I've never seen one myself, but I've heard them described."

I looked at him, confused by his concern. "It's just a dog," I said. "Actually, it's the dog that woke me up after my crash. He was making out with my face and—" I waved it off. "Never mind. The point is he's harmless." I offered the dog the back of my hand. "Come here, boy."

"Rude," said the dog. *"You want me to just call you 'girl'? No, I don't think so."*

"Oh, my bad. Do you have a name?"

He plopped his big butt down on the cobblestone. *"No. But that's not the point."*

"What's the point?"

Tanner cleared his throat. "Um," he said cautiously. "Are you, uh, I don't know how to say this without being insulting. Are you having a conversation with that hound?"

I looked from Tanner to the dog and then back to Tanner. "Yeah. I mean, it's not *great* conversation. He has a little bit of an attitude." I muttered the last bit from the corner of my mouth so the dog wouldn't overhear.

Tanner took a step back. "Ah. Okay. So here's what *I'm* seeing." Why was he speaking to me like I was crazy? Sure, a talking dog was weird, but I'd just had a conversation with the grim reaper about bridge. A talking dog seemed fairly normal in comparison.

Tanner continued. "I'm seeing you say things to that big furry beast, and then the big furry beast is responding by growling in a not-entirely-friendly way."

I held up a hand to stop him and shut my eyes, trying to wrap my mind around it. "You're telling me you can't hear him speaking?"

Tanner shook his head, and I turned to the dog. "Why can't he hear you speaking?"

"Aw poop," said the dog. He flopped down and set his head on his paws. *"This can't be happening."*

Tanner gasped. "I know what's going on! Except ... I've never heard of it being a dog. Oh wait! No, I have! But just once."

"Care to clue me in? Either one of you?"

Tanner cackled. "Ha! I was right! You *are* a witch!"

"You're not exactly filling in the blanks," I said, losing patience.

"He's your familiar!" he explained. "Every witch has a familiar. It's an animal that connects with your magic. You can communicate with each other. That's why you can hear him but I can't."

"Huh. You have a familiar, too?"

"Yeah. She prefers to be a house cat, though, and refuses to come to work with me since so much of the clientele are werewolves."

"Huh," I said again, staring down at the dog, who

didn't seem particularly excited about the prospect. "I've always wanted a pet."

"Not your pet," corrected the dog. *"I don't do the domestication thing. Sorry not sorry."*

Tanner crouched down, facing the dog who was still ten yards off. "Hey there, buddy! Who's a good doggie? You want to come with us?"

The dog stood up slowly. *"Okay, first of all, not cool. But also,* I'm *a good doggie."* He trotted over, his tail wagging lethargically. *"This guy gets to pet me this one time, then that's it, okay?"*

"Whatever you say," I said, biting my lip so I didn't laugh at the dog's lack of self-control.

"There's a good boy," Tanner crooned as he scratched behind the dog's ears.

The hound groaned. *"Oh yeah ... that's the spot. A little to the left."*

I relayed the message to Tanner, who indulged.

As the dog sat stock still, letting Tanner continue with the scratches, he shot me serious side-eye. *"You tell no one what you've seen here."*

"My lips are sealed."

The dog kicked his leg, thumping the ground with his massive paw when Tanner found the sweet spot behind his big, black ears. *"Gnuhhhh,"* the dog moaned.

Okay, this was officially crossing into uncomfortable territory. "Should I leave you two alone?" I said, cringing.

The implication wasn't immediately obvious to Tanner, but it clicked before long. He yanked his hand away and lurched back from the dog.

"Definitely didn't think about it like that," he said.

"It was totally platonic! Oh come on!"

* * *

"You're going to love Ruby," Tanner said as we climbed the front porch steps up to her attached cottage.

Tanner had played the role of tour guide on our hike, explaining that the fountain we passed in Fulcrum Park was spring fed and marked the center of Eastwind, and that, come morning, the Eastwind Emporium, an empty lot except for a tall clock tower, would become a bustling farmer's market. I hadn't been able to make out many of the details of the tall, old buildings that rose up on either side of us as we made our way through the streets of Eastwind, but I saw just enough to know the place would be like a wonderful fairy tale in the daylight. No matter what the next day brought, I was determined to do a little sightseeing around town once I had a few hours of sleep in me.

I wasn't great about taking vacations. That probably doesn't come as a surprise. But I'd always wanted to do the backpacking in Europe thing. Of course, my friends who'd done that—taken a year off before college or taken a semester off during—all had generous benefactors financing their quests to "find themselves"; namely, their parents. I didn't have that. And I didn't think taking on ten thousand dollars more in debt was the smartest thing when I wasn't sure what life might hold after culinary school (already an expensive endeavor).

I'd always regretted it, though, and every time a friend returned with pictures from this small Italian village or that quaint Dutch fishing town, my heart ached.

Here I was, though, in a town that looked like every

little Belgian or German village I'd ever seen ... and my mind was set on finding a way to leave? Just because the place was teeming with supernatural creatures that could tear me to shreds? Please. I'd faced more danger taking the bus around Austin.

And besides, I had Tanner. He wouldn't let anything happen to me. Hopefully.

He rapped three times on the door with the knocker then, as if he'd forgotten something, he startled and quickly added a fourth knock. "Ruby doesn't like it when you knock three times. 'Only dark things knock thrice!' she always says."

"She sounds lovely."

I wondered about Tanner's sarcasm radar, because he nodded enthusiastically and said, "Totally."

The dog settled himself on the porch, curling into a tight ball and placing his snout on his paws.

When the door swung open, a tiny gray-haired woman stared at us through icy blue eyes. She was easily in her seventies, and donned a midnight blue nightgown and overstuffed slippers that were made to look like large paws, not unlike those on my alleged familiar, except hers were red. She spared only a brief glance for Tanner, and when she turned her gaze my direction, her eyes focused on the space around me rather than looking directly at me. Finally, she nodded. "I suppose I have the Fifth Wind to thank for this! Get in here, you two. The dog stays out, though."

"I had no plans on entering into the strange lady's house, anyway," mumbled the dog. *"It's called survival instinct."*

"The dog is Nora's familiar, though," said Tanner. "Shouldn't he—"

Ruby cut him off. "Not without a bath, he shouldn't." She took two hurried steps forward so that Tanner and I had to move to the side to avoid her running into us.

Her head swiveled, scanning the dark street, then she seemed satisfied and motioned rapidly with her arm for us to enter.

The interior of the townhouse was dim, lit only by a glowing fireplace and two lamps—one on a wall sconce in the connected kitchen, the other glowing atop an old wooden table at the center of the parlor into which we immediately found ourselves upon entering her home. The light reflected off the myriad objects hanging from the ceiling—brass and silver and marble bells, dream catchers, tiny wood carvings on the end of chains, a crucifix, and two dozen other unidentifiable knick-knacks. I walked underneath them hesitantly, unsure of their purpose. A few hung low enough that I had to duck to keep from getting whopped in the face. None came close to the top of Ruby's head, though, and she shuffled through the parlor, grabbing the lamp from the table as she passed on her way towards a narrow staircase at the opposite side of the room. "You'll be upstairs. Follow me."

I did, and Tanner came along, which I was grateful for, since this place gave me a raging case of the creeps.

The stairs creaked underfoot as we ascended to the second floor, passed a door at the landing, and headed up an additional flight to the third story. The stairs dead-ended at a heavy wooden door with a rusty metal handle, and Ruby had to shove with two hands to get the thing to budge. It opened laboriously, and I peeked inside, concerned about what I might find.

But as it turned out, her spare bedroom didn't carry over the aesthetic of the rest of the house. The wood floors looked new, and the walls were light—I couldn't tell exactly what hue in the darkness, but I was able to see that they weren't dark like the rest of the house.

On the far side of the room was a big window overlooking the street. The curtains were pulled back and moonlight streamed in. I chuckled, thinking of how much money my friends might've dropped to stay in an Airbnb like this in France or The Netherlands.

Yeah, this would do.

"Bathroom is on the first floor. I make a pot of tea at seven sharp each morning. I eat a slice of toast with jam and two strips of bacon every morning, and I'm happy to make extra if you would like some."

"That sounds perfect. Thanks so much, Ru—"

"Sleep well, and if you hear something knock thrice on your bedroom door, for the sake of earthly things, don't answer it!" She turned and ambled from the room, leaving me with my mouth hanging open. I turned to Tanner. "Is she serious?"

"Oh yeah," he said. "Ruby knows what she's talking about."

I thought about the random objects suspended from the parlor ceiling. "Does she? Because it looks a little like an aerial version of *Hoarders* downstairs." As soon as it was out of my mouth, I knew Tanner would be lost. "Forget it. I promise I won't answer the door if something knocks three times. Oh, I'm sorry, *thrice*. Mostly because

I plan on passing out so hard Ruby might have half a mind to round up Ted to collect me."

"I hear that. I'm so beat I don't even know if I'll make it home before blacking out."

My eyes flickered over to the queen-size four-poster bed, and the opportunist in me perked up. "I would hate for you to fall asleep and get eaten by some werewolf or another ..." I smiled gently at him, eyebrows arched, inviting him to fill in the blank.

"Oh, um." He cleared his throat quickly. "No, I think I'll be fine. I'm friends with most of the weres in town anyway. Heh." He grinned broadly. "Well ... it was nice meeting you, Nora. See you soon?"

Dang. Shut down. "Yeah. It was nice to meet you too, Tanner. Maybe I'll stop by for lunch tomorrow."

His smokey eyes brightened. "That would be awesome!"

I hadn't completely scared him with my subtle pass then. That was a small victory. I guess I could always use a friend. A beautiful, beautiful friend.

"Night," he said. "Um ..." He offered his hand.

Oof. A goodnight handshake? Talk about salt in the wound.

But I went with it. Only, when I put my hand in his, he didn't shake but brought my hand to his face and planted a soft kiss on the back of it.

A rush of dizziness surged through me.

Please don't let this be a platonic custom in Eastwind, I thought.

He stared up at me as his lips parted from my skin, and ... What the heck was *that* look? I mean, I *knew* that look. I'd seen it in the eyes of men before, just not any men who'd, only seconds previous, parried my invite to spend the night before it even got started. Could he actually be as interested as that look implied?

Sheesh, if he were a werewolf, I might have thought he wanted to eat me with the hunger in those hazel eyes.

I remembered to breathe again as he let go of my hand and headed toward to the door to leave.

"Tanner," I said quickly.

He paused and turned. "Yeah?" There was a note of hope in his voice, and I had this feeling that if I'd asked him to stay just then, he would've said yes.

But I didn't. "Your coat." I slipped it off, and his intense expression softened.

"Oh, right."

I handed over the heavy article, and he grinned at me and left without another word.

Chapter Five

I startled awake but couldn't pinpoint a cause. I hadn't had a nightmare, hadn't heard knocking on the door (thank god), and the room was still dark, so sunlight hadn't been the culprit. Yet, I was *wide* awake.

Every particle of my body stood at attention, like a new sense had awoken in me. It wasn't quite touch, but it felt something like that, only internally. My body was sending clear signals to my brain of *something is here.* I stared at the ceiling, already knowing to some extent what I would find when I sat up and looked over at the easy chair in the corner of the room. I didn't know how I knew it, but I knew that I knew it.

And now I sound like an insane person.

Just wait, though, it gets worse.

With an effort, I slid up on the bed until my back was against the headboard, and I confronted the man sitting in the chair. "Hi."

He grinned, and I felt a little less petrified. It was the same grin he'd offered me when I'd first stepped into

Medium Rare. Except now it was slightly translucent. "I apologize for dropping in. I would have knocked, but ..." He held up his hands, which thinned like smoke with the movement, then became more distinct once motion ceased.

"I wouldn't have answered anyway," I replied honestly.

"It's a shame we have to meet this way. The moment I saw you walk through the door, when you paused to take in the smells of the diner, I thought, there's a woman I'd like to get to know."

This was, of course, a lot for me to take in. For one, I was absolutely sure that I was speaking to a ghost. I mean, okay, I did consider the possibility that I was insane, like bat-scat crazy. But here's the thing: insane people don't usually know they're insane. So whether my brain had been jostled in my skull when I ran my car into a tree or whether this was actually happening the way I saw it happening sort of became irrelevant. This was my reality, even if it wasn't real. So I decided to embrace it. For now.

The one thing I *wouldn't* embrace, though, was Bruce's sleaziness. "If you could just cut to the chase, that would be fantastic. I'd like to get a little more sleep, and it's already creepy enough that you floated your way into here to watch me sleep *without* the added layer of you coming on to me."

He held up his ghostly hands in mock surrender. "Fair enough. I need your help."

I nodded once, trying not to show how relieved I was that his answer hadn't been, "I'm here to kill you."

Why did that exist in my mind as a possibility? Perhaps because I'd just woken up in a strange, dark room with a ghost creeping on me, so my rational thinking was not at its peak. Cut me some slack.

"I don't know why you think I'm the gal for the job," I said. "I don't know anything about you or this weird town."

"You're my gal because you're the only person in this *weird town* who I can communicate with."

"Wait, really?"

"Well, technically there's one other person, but she doesn't want to be bothered. That means you're it."

"So you want my help because I'm literally your only option."

"You got it."

"Huh." I paused, staring down at the fleur-de-lis bedspread. "I don't know how I feel about that." I looked up at him. "It's kind of insulting, honestly."

"So is being murdered," he said dryly.

"Touché. Speaking of which, care to tell me who did it so I can pass the word along to Deputy Manchester?"

He cringed. "Yeah, see, that's the thing. I don't know who did it. I never got a look."

"That sucks."

"Tell me about it."

Now that the initial shock was wearing off, my eyelids grew heavy. "How about this. You let me get a few hours more sleep, and I'll get started on solving your murder—despite having absolutely no experience in this sort of thing—in the morning."

He rubbed his chin, except his fingertips went through the space where his chin appeared. "Fair enough."

"Oh, and one more thing," I added.

He nodded expectantly. "Yes?"

"Promise you won't continue watching me while I sleep."

"I think you have the wrong impression of me," he protested.

"If so, it's only because that's the impression you give off."

"You're a feisty one, aren't you?" He grinned, and his nostrils flared, despite being unable to actually inhale.

"If you want me to stop thinking you're a cad, stop acting like one."

I scooted my butt down in bed, flopped back onto my pillow, and pulled the covers up over my head.

He took the hint, and when I peeked over at the chair a moment later, it was empty.

"You look terrible," Ruby said the next morning in lieu of a proper greeting. I lumbered into the parlor at seven thirty, according to the analog clock on my bedside table, hoping I hadn't missed tea. I needed tea. Lots of it. She stood with her back to me as she topped up her cup and poured me one as well. She no longer wore her midnight blue nightgown, dressing instead in multiple layers of plain robes, each a more washed-out shade of brown than the next. The loose fabric of them swished around her ankles as she shuffled around the kitchen, which was hardly more than a nook of the large parlor, which itself seemed to make up the majority of the first floor.

Tea would be nice, though what I could *really* use was a double espresso. But *if* this town made those,

Ruby's was not the likely place to find one. She struck me as the type of person to drink the same kind of tea every morning for her entire life.

"I didn't get the best sleep last night," I said, feeling for some reason that I owed her an explanation for my disheveled appearance. "And I usually shower first thing in the morning."

"Oh, we don't shower here," Ruby said, her back still to me. "Waste of water."

"Ew," I said impulsively. "I mean, um ..."

"No, no, I thought the same thing at first. But it's much better this way. Magic does the trick just as well. I'll show you after breakfast. Don't even need to undress."

I was intrigued and, I'll admit, relieved that I wouldn't have to undress anywhere in the downstairs of her home. The place with all its dangling totems still gave me the heebie-jeebies.

"Bacon might be a little cold by now, but help yourself," she said as I scooted out a heavy wooden chair at the parlor table, the legs scraping noisily over her dry wooden floors.

Then, as I reached for a piece of bacon (crispy, just the way I love it) plated at the center of the table, she added, as if nothing more than small talk, "Was it Bruce Saxon?"

My dire need for caffeine lessened just a smidgen as her mention of my late-night visitor jolted me from my mental fog. "Yes. How did you guess?"

She brought over the tea and set it in front of me then scooted out her chair without a sound, sitting gracefully for her old age. "Because he tried me first. I told him to get lost, of course, because I'm out of the game of helping everyone solve the problems they create for themselves. I told him to check down the hall if he needed a shoulder to cry on. Sounds like he listened."

"I don't understand."

Ruby eyed me boldly over the lip of her teacup as she tilted it back, sipping lightly. Slowly, she set it down on the saucer, cradling it between her hands. "I suppose there's no way around this. I can't very well retire, not properly, without training a replacement."

"A replacement for what?"

She sighed. "I've been Eastwind's go-to psychic medium since I stumbled into this place myself about, oh, close to fifty years ago? Don't take that as bragging about my own abilities. The main reason I've been the go-to medium is that I've been the only medium. Until now." She smiled at me, deep lines stretching out from the corners of her eyes. "My attempt at retiring hasn't been the most successful up to this point, but now here you are. And *you* can be the one who gets harangued night and day by those who can't take death's hint and scoot along beyond the veil."

I wasn't sure if I'd heard her right. Because from what I understood, she'd just implied I was a psychic medium. And while I admit that seeing Bruce the night before could be construed as corroborating evidence, I was pretty sure I would've had ghost encounters prior to last night if I were actually a medium.

Plus, this town had fauns. Couldn't it also have ghosts running around that everyone could see? Weird is weird, right?

"I'm not a psychic," I said. To be fair, I really wanted that to be the truth, and I thought saying it might help bring that into being. I think Oprah said something about that, right? Your thoughts bring things into being? Well, I'd rarely had time to watch Oprah, so I'd mostly gleaned that idea from the servers around me, who regurgitated it whenever I was being particularly cynical. "I'm not anything special. I'm just a human, and I really need to figure out how to get home."

Ruby tilted her head gently to the side and smiled sadly at me. "Oh dear, you're never getting home. I'm sorry to be the one to tell you that."

And I thought *I* could be cynical sometimes. Sheesh. "I have to get home. I have a business to run and a—"

She'd been sipping her tea when I started talking, but slowly she lowered her cup and cleared her throat, cutting me off. "Witches may come and go from Eastwind as they please ... so long as they don't enter on the Fifth Wind, as was the case for you."

"I'm sorry. I don't mean to be impolite—after all, you opened your home to me when I came wandering into town—but you're going to have to back up a few steps here. Explain it to me like I'm an idiot."

She smiled, but I sensed impatience behind it. "Of course. There are four winds that everyone, regardless of species, can feel blow against their skin. The North Wind, the South Wind, the West Wind, and, the namesake of our dangerous yet beloved town, the East Wind. Each one is associated with a season and an element. And each witch can harness one of those winds and all its strengths. But while you are most definitely a witch, you aren't a pyromancer of the South Wind or an aeromancer of the North Wind. You, Nora, are master of none of the four winds."

I refrained from sarcastically saying, "You mean because I'm not a witch?"

She continued. "You're of the Fifth Wind, of that chill you feel on your skin that comes from no earthly direction. Witches like you and me are rare, mostly because we're so powerful, but also because we're so tricky to create. May I ask you something personal, Nora?"

Was this not already personal? It sure as heck felt personal. The woman knew more about me than I did. "Sure."

"What is the last thing you remember before you woke up in Eastwind?"

"I was driving down the road, and I passed a sign for Eastwind, Texas, and—"

She held up a hand and I stopped with my mouth hanging open. "Actually," she said, "how about I tell *you* the last thing I remember before I woke up in Eastwind."

"You weren't born here?"

She shook her head. "I'm from Illinois. It was February. I was twenty-nine years old, driving home after visiting a gentleman friend. Eastwind, Illinois, was one of the small towns I passed through on my way." She sipped her tea as her focus drifted to the air above my head, and the lines around her eyes softened with calm nostalgia. "I could hardly see three feet ahead of me through the snow, so I was driving cautiously, but not cautiously enough, it seemed. Suddenly, a dark figure appeared in the road ahead. In that split second between when I spotted it and when I swerved, I was so utterly confused. Amid all the white, it was jet black. And it stood there like it was expecting me. It didn't move a muscle as my car headed straight for it." She shook her head slightly and her eyes refocused on me. "I hit something, I couldn't tell what in the white out, and the next thing I knew, I woke up on the edge of the Outskirts and the snow was gone. So was my Studebaker. Sound familiar?"

Whoa, doggy. I didn't know what to say. Yes, it sounded familiar.

Okay, so maybe I would listen to what Ruby had to say. She might actually know a thing or two. "You've been here ever since?"

"Yes. And slowly I discovered the ability that you now have. I could see ghosts."

I scrunched up my face. "That's not a thing everyone can do?"

"No, Nora. It's not. The only living people who can see ghosts at this point, that I know about, are sitting at this table."

"Dang."

Ruby rolled her eyes. "You have no idea. But let me ask you something. Before you came here, did you have a family?"

I shook my head quickly.

"What about a boyfriend?"

I thought of Neil, then I shook my head again.

"And let me guess, you never felt like you belonged anywhere that existed in that world. You felt compelled to create somewhere for yourself where you were integral to it, where you belonged. Somewhere that couldn't function without you."

The hustle and clatter of Chez Coeur floated around my mind. "You're good at this."

She waved that off with a flick of her wrist. "It's not

that hard to guess. You felt like you didn't belong and you didn't anchor yourself there with romance or a family because that wasn't where you were meant to be. Your life was leading you here. And I know that's a lot to digest at present, but I speak from almost fifty years of experience in this town. This is where you're supposed to be. This town has a place waiting for you. It's where you're supposed to settle down, meet a nice man." She arched an eyebrow at me slowly, drawing it out.

The memory of Tanner setting two plates of pie in front of me surfaced. I could practically smell the warm crust, the way it made me feel, like I had just come home after a lifelong business trip.

"Got any coffee?" a man's voice said, cutting through my reverie. "I'm not much of a tea drinker."

The spirit of Bruce Saxon walked into the parlor, passing straight through the front door of the True residence.

"You're not much of an anything drinker now, Bruce. You're dead," Ruby reminded him.

She pulled out a chair at the table since he couldn't do it himself, and he sat, his butt sinking through the wooden surfaces slightly. He crossed his arms over his chest. "Well, shoot. I guess you're right. I keep forgetting."

"I assume we can help you with something else," said Ruby.

"Such as?" he said, then he remembered before Ruby could respond. "Oh right! My murder. Yes, yes. I need you to figure out who killed me."

He'd addressed Ruby, but she shook her head and

pointed to me. "I've already told you, Bruce. I'm retired. That's your girl, now."

I pointed to myself dumbly. "Me? I already told him I don't know anything about solving murders."

"Great," mumbled Bruce morosely.

"You absolutely do, dear," Ruby said. "It's part of the gig. As a master of the Fifth Wind, you have a strong connection to the stars. You can read the signs."

"You mean astrology?" I asked dubiously. I'm not sure why, after everything I'd seen and heard since entering Eastwind, astrology was the straw that broke the camel's back when it came to my suspension of disbelief.

"Sort of like that, except you haven't *studied* astrology. It's a complicated science that takes years to master. What doesn't take years of study, though, is your intuition and logical reasoning. You're able to spot patterns well. One day that will allow you to learn divination, but for the time being, it just makes you a little smarter than the average witch in these kinds of situations."

"Let me get this straight," I said. "I can't do all the fun witch stuff you see in movies, and instead, I have to be a private investigator witch?"

"That's about the long and short of it. Glad to see you're finally catching on."

I turned to Bruce. "If I refuse to help you, what will you do then?"

He shrugged his translucent shoulders. "Haunt you, I guess. I got nothing but time now."

I glanced at Ruby, who gave me a look as if to say, "See what I've been dealing with?"

I groaned, took a long drink of my tea, then relented.

"Fine. What's the last thing you remember before your death?" I ignored Ruby's almost imperceptible fist pump.

"I was almost done making a steak in the kitchen of Medium Rare, when I could've sworn I heard the back door of the restaurant slam. I thought it was Tanner, but then a second later, he charged in the kitchen making a beeline for the employee bathrooms that were in the same direction as the back door.

"I'd been hearing strange noises in the days leading up to that, but those were more garbled hums and whines, sometimes mumbling voices, not loud slams. So I put the steak on a plate with the eggs and went to investigate. I walked around the kitchen, looked in the storage and the freezer, but didn't see anything. Then I went to check my office, and then ... all black."

I looked at Ruby, who was clearly struggling to keep her mouth shut. Retirement must not be second nature to her yet.

I tried to think back to the few episodes of Law & Order I'd watched in my spare time.

They were no help.

But I did remember one tidbit that was useful: means, motive, and opportunity. A killer would have all three.

"Do you know of anyone who would want you dead?" I asked.

Bruce thought about it, screwing up his face like he was in pain. "I don't think so. I mean, I know Jane hates me, but I didn't think she'd want to kill me. She was more the type to want me to suffer. Death would be too easy."

"Who's Jane?" I asked.

"My ex-wife."

I glanced at Ruby, who nodded.

"Okay. I'll start there, I guess. Where can I find her?"

"She's a manager over at the little pizzeria downtown. Franco's Pizza, I think it's called. She used to manage at Medium Rare, but obviously, that was no longer a viable option when she stopped loving me and started hating me. When people in this town want comfort food, they either go to Medium Rare or they go to Franco's Pizza. They're our biggest competition, for sure. She could've gotten a job at any of the dozens of little cafes or restaurants around town, but she went there, and I'm absolutely certain it was to spite me. She knew I'd want her to work anywhere *but* Franco's Pizza."

"And your ex-wife. She's a ..." I let the sentence hang, not wanting to be rude by asking what kind of creature she was.

"Bitch," he said plainly.

"That's not very nice," I said.

"Huh?" He seemed genuinely confused. "It's true, though. She's a female werewolf."

"They're called bitches around here," Ruby said gently. "I know, it took a bit for me to get used to it, too."

I looked back and forth between the two, wondering if I was being messed with. "Okay. Um, I hope it's alright if I just call them female werewolves."

Bruce shrugged like he couldn't care less.

I finished the last of my tea. "I guess I'm off then." I stood from the table.

Ruby did as well. "Not before you clean up a bit, dear."

"Oh right."

"You"—she pointed to Bruce—"wait here. And you"—she pointed to me—"follow me."

59

She led me into the bathroom, which was remarkably clean. I'd expected it to be grimy, given the state of the rest of the downstairs, although, when I thought about it more, nothing downstairs was unclean, it was just old, dim, and those things hanging from the ceiling ... yuck. They seriously gave me the creeps.

"Step under here," she said, motioning toward a small enclave that looked remarkably similar to a shower, except without a drain.

I started to take off my overcoat.

"Nope," she said. "You keep that on. You won't get wet. Eastwind doesn't waste water the same way our home world does."

"Oh, um. Okay."

Where a showerhead would have existed in a normal shower, a smooth wooden knob protruded from the wall, just above my head.

"Now what?" I asked.

"Now nothing. Just give it a minute to decide how to approach your particular kind of filth."

"Oh gee, that's lovely."

Suddenly, it felt like warm sunlight touched every inch of my body. The sensation was invigorating and accompanied by the scent of lilies and something else ...

"The scent of sage is just part of it," Ruby said, as if reading my mind. "Side effect of witch-made magical items. But it'll wear off once you air out a bit."

"That's it?" I look down at my clothes, which were suddenly wrinkle-free, despite having slept in both the shirt and trousers for lack of other options.

"That's it. And I got a hose out back that works just

like it, if you get around to bathing that stinky familiar of yours."

"Noted," I said, though I was distracted by my reflection in the mirror. My greasy hair was suddenly fresh and full of body. "There's a good chance the past twelve hours have been an extended hallucination," I said, running a finger through my clean hair, "but if that's the case, I'll take it so long as it means I get things like magical showers."

She chuckled. "If you don't watch out, Eastwind will spoil a girl like you. I know, because it spoiled a girl like me for a solid ten years before I managed to get over myself."

Ruby led me back into the parlor and then said, "I'd better feed Clifford."

"Who?" I asked.

"Clifford. My familiar."

"You have a familiar?"

Ruby and Bruce shared a condescending glance at my expense. "Yes," she said. "All witches do. Clifford isn't an early riser, though. He seems more intent on retirement than I am. But he gets a little cranky if he goes without breakfast."

"Clifford," I said. I remembered her slippers from the night before. "Is he by any chance big and red?"

Bruce looked confused, but Ruby nodded. "Ah yes, it *is* nice to have someone around who understands my references. Yes, you guessed right. He's big and red. Or at least he used to be red. Now he's mostly gray." She made for the staircase but paused and snapped her fingers when she remembered something. "I should probably teach you how to anchor."

"How to what?"

Instead of answering me, she scurried over to the kitchen, pulled out a copper bowl, and a few small, wooden boxes with carvings on the top, which she stacked one on top of another and brought to the parlor table.

Setting the things down next to my tea, she opened the boxes one by one, revealing a rich, earthy scent of dried herbs. "You may not be a terramancer, but you can do a few things. Most useful is the anchoring spell. Forget to do it, and you'll have these types"—she nodded at Bruce without taking her eyes off the herbs—"following you everywhere you go." She took a pinch from each of the boxes, crushing the leaves and stems between her fingers before sprinkling them around the copper bowl. Then she looked up to make sure I was paying attention. "Trust me when I say that gets old quick. Besides, just because someone's dead doesn't mean they're suddenly self-reflective and wise. Their inability to accurately judge the character of others can affect your rational thinking when it comes to finding a killer."

"I don't have bad judgment!" Bruce protested.

Ruby nodded at him. "See? He doesn't even know. I can't tell you how many times people are killed by those they trusted. They don't see who killed them because the murderer couldn't stand to see the look of betrayal on the victim's face. Then they show up here rather than crossing over. "

She opened a small round box which contrasted the rectangular and hexagonal shapes of the others, and pulled out three berries. "Night veils. You need to crush these with the sage, mint, and rosemary, but not with your fingers. The juice is hard to wash off, and a drop of it can be fatal." She opened the last box, a long rectangular one, and inside was a copper pestle. She pulled it out, careful not to touch the end, which was stained a midnight blue, presumably from the night veil berries.

As she crushed the contents of the copper bowl into a paste, she instructed me to look around the room, to soak in as much detail as possible, then close my eyes and construct the space in my imagination. As I did so, she grabbed my hand, holding it over the bowl.

A sudden blast of cold traveled up my fingertips, enveloping my entire hand to the wrist. Then, just as quickly, it passed.

"You can open your eyes," she said.

She set the bowl in the center of the table, knocked the excess off the pestle, and then placed it gently in the box. "There. Now he's anchored. Thank you for your compliance, Bruce. I know my home isn't the most fascinating of places to spend your time hovering between planes, but obviously, if you want Nora's help, you have to play by the rules." She gathered the boxes, replacing them on the kitchen shelf. "Leave the bowl there, dear," she said to me. "And he'll be here until you return. I'll show you how to release the anchor later, if you need." She clapped her hands quickly. "Oh, and before I forget." She reached into a pocket of her baggy layers of clothing and pulled out a small, bulging leather pouch, offering it me. "You'll need a little bit of money to navigate around town." The purse clanked as she passed it off. The heavy weight of it surprised me, and I wondered how much this could actually buy me around Eastwind.

"Now, I better feed Clifford before he comes out here and eats you."

I stuffed the coins into the pocket of my overcoat. "Clifford eats people?"

She shrugged. "Not regularly, but yes, it has happened. I can't say I blame him. If you'd encountered that pugnacious gnome, you might have found a way to eat him, too. Filthy mouth on that one."

"And this dog sleeps in your room with you?"

"Of course. Oh, but you don't know ... Familiars cannot harm the witch they serve. And if you want that mangy familiar of yours to sleep indoors, all you need to do is bathe him. Then he's welcome inside. I'm sure Clifford would appreciate the company. Up until last night, he was the only non-cat familiar in Eastwind."

"I'll let the dog know." With one last look at Bruce then the copper bowl anchoring him to Ruby True's house, I turned and headed out, wondering how long it would take to find Franco's Pizza.

Chapter Six

"You again," said the black dog as soon as I shut the front door of Ruby's house behind me.

"Yep. Me again. And I have a name. It's Nora."

The dog lumbered to his feet slowly before stretching. *"Brag about it, why don't you?"*

"You really don't have a name?"

"No. Why would I? I'm a dog. You're the only non-dog I've ever spoken to."

I descended the steps off the porch and the dog followed. "Dogs don't give each other names?" I asked.

"Nope. We don't need them. We pretty much just say, 'hey you!' whenever we need someone. It gets the job done. But I don't talk to them anymore. Or I guess I should say they don't talk to me anymore. Not since I died."

I stopped in my tracks and stared down at him. "You're a ghost dog?"

If you've never seen a dog roll his eyes, it's quite something. *"No. I'm not a ghost dog. I'm a grim hound."*

"I'll say. I've never met a grimmer hound."

"*No, not—well, okay, maybe I'm a little grim. But I'm also a grim.*"

"Meaning?" I knew I should get going to the pizzeria, but this had my full attention. And it wasn't like Bruce was getting any deader.

"*Meaning I was just a regular hellhound, living life to the fullest out in the Deadwoods, and then I died—long story—but it turned out I was a grim without knowing it, so I didn't die. I was buried underground and then I rose again.*"

"Like Jesus?"

He shook his shaggy head. "*Depends. Is he a grim?*"

"No, I'm fairly sure not."

"*The point is, all hounds can sense ghosts, but only grims can* see *them. So once I came back and let the others know I could now see ghosts running around, they wanted nothing to do with me. Which is just fine by me. They were stupid idiots anyway.*"

That explained the attitude. "So, should I give you a name?"

"*As long as it's not a stupid one like—*"

"Grim," I said.

"*I was literally about to say Grim.*"

"I like that one. It fits you."

He growled. "*It's a tad on-the-snout.*"

"I don't know about that," I said. And hey, I was getting satisfaction out of his annoyance. Sue me. "Okay, Grim. Do you know where Franco's Pizza is?"

He growled again.

"What? You don't know?"

"*You're not calling me Grim.*"

"Oh, I am," I said. "Just watch."

A young girl trotted by, and I hollered, "Morning!" Once I had her attention, I added, "I'm Nora, and this is my dog, Grim."

She waved. "Hi, Nora! Hi, Grim! I'm Felicia!" Then she continued on her way, clip-clopping down the cobblestone street.

Oh right, I should mention that she was only a girl from the waist up. The bottom half? All goat. A faun seemed normal after the last twenty-four hours, though.

"See?" I said. "Unless you can tell them otherwise, your name is Grim."

Grim growled low and deep. *Well played. And for the record, if you continue carrying on a conversation with me aloud, people will think you've lost your mind.*

"Is this your sneaky way of getting me to stop talking to you?"

No, but that's smart. I just mean I can hear your thoughts.

Oh no, I thought. *Did he overhear it when I was thinking about how hot Tanner is?*

I didn't before. But I did just now.

"What?"

From what I can tell, you have to direct the thoughts at me, or focus on me when you think them.

"Noted. I apologize in advance if you overhear something personal by accident."

"More personal than you having the hots for Tanner?"

"Oh yes, Grim. It gets quite dark inside this head of mine."

He wagged his tail. *"Now there's something I can relate to."*

Just as I'd expected, Eastwind in the daytime was

magical. As we walked down a narrow side street sloping sharply up toward Fulcrum Park, buildings on either side of us bustled with activity, each one a different bright color from its neighbors.

Even as I followed Grim through the crowd of creatures that, had you told me they existed two days before, would have caused me to gently suggest to your loved ones that you be committed somewhere with white, padded walls, I couldn't help but feel ... dare I say it?

Happy.

I felt happy. Almost euphoric. There was an energy in this town that I'd never experienced. Everyone, every*thing* was so full of life. Bursting with it. Had other towns felt this way before and I'd just missed it?

I wasn't sure how big Eastwind was, but only a dozen or so townsfolk stopped in their tracks to stare at me as I passed. Everyone else must have been too engrossed in their own morning errands to worry about some strange woman and her dingy black dog cutting down the center of the road, passing by this butcher shop and that salon. It was all too much to take in. There were so many new things—sights, sounds, smells.

As the sun began to warm the February air, I unbuttoned my overcoat and felt the fresh air swirl around me. From what I'd seen, Eastwind didn't have any cars. Did it have factories? Oil refineries? My mind traveled to the magical shower, and I suspected that if Eastwind had ever gone down the path of air pollution, it'd long since replaced those things with earth-friendly magical solutions. And it showed. I'd never smelled air so crisp and clean.

After what I judged to be about twenty minutes of

walking, every second of which I enjoyed, the street opened to the wide circle of the Eastwind Emporium with the clock tower at the center. The rest of the space was, as Tanner said it would be, packed with one cart after another offering fruits or vegetables or herbs or nuts. It was a farmer's market like I'd never seen before. Again, the colors were breathtaking. The tomatoes were ruby red, the spinach emerald green.

Following Grim, I passed a cart with more types of berries than I knew existed. Some I recognized—blueberries, raspberries, mulberries—but mostly I was dumbfounded. One woven basket spilled over with plump gold berries. Not yellow or orange. Gold. Like, shiny gold that glittered in the sunlight. The merchant was small and hovered a few feet off the ground, sparkling wings moving rapidly behind her like a hummingbird's. I hated to stereotype, but I'd have put money on her being a fairy.

"Don't be shy," she said congenially. "Sample away!"

She didn't have to tell me twice. The chef in me was in heaven. Every new berry represented an array of brand-new dishes. How long had it been since I'd sampled a new flavor of anything? My palate had grown complacent over time, having spent years sampling every new taste I could get my hands on, from nuts grown only in Southeast Asian jungles to bark nestled in the foothills of the Andes.

I tried one of everything from the cart, even the things I could name. The raspberries were sweeter than any I'd tasted and reminded me of a crisp spring I used to swim in just outside of Austin. And the cherries. Oh, god help me! The cherries burst with more flavor than I knew cherries could! Not to take away from Tanner's baking abilities, but it seemed almost impossible to mess up cherry pie if you started with berries like these.

I'd just gotten to the gold berries, which tasted ... well, I don't have vocabulary for them, but the closest thing I can think of is "sunbeams," when someone tugged on the back of my overcoat. I turned to find the black fabric tucked between Grim's slobbery lips.

"Let's get going, or you'll spend all day there," he said telepathically. It was convenient that he didn't actually have to move his mouth to communicate since it was full of my clothes.

I shoved him off of me and followed. *"I wouldn't have spent all day there,"* I said. *"I have self-control. I'm an adult."*

"So say you. Except look at the clock."

"Huh?" I looked up at the clock in the center of the market. Wait. But how?

It'd been nearly forty-five minute since I'd last checked it, though it'd felt more like three.

"Typical sales tactic," Grim explained. *"That fairy sprinkles a little bit of her special dust on the produce, you lose time, and her cart looks extra busy, which attracts more paying customers who think it must be good."*

"That doesn't seem ethical."

"It's not. Did you expect marketing to be ethical? Surely that can't be the case, not even in your old boring home world."

Franco's Pizza was right off the farmer's market, a few dozen yards down a side street. A red-and-white striped awning hung over the dark green front door. I could smell the tomato sauce as soon as we entered the alley and wondered how many other things from my world had made it into Eastwind with people like me who'd entered.

But then I had a strange thought.

What if the stuff I know to be Italian food was actually started in Eastwind and then passed along to the world I knew? Could that mean people were able to travel back and forth, contrary to what Ruby said?

"You going in, or you just going to sit out here all day like a prowler?" Grim said.

I glared down at him. *"Oh, by the way, Ruby said you're welcome to come into her house and meet her familiar, Clifford, if you let me bathe you."*

"I don't need you to bathe me," he said gruffly. *"I'm not your pet. And I've managed it myself my whole life."*

I leaned forward, reaching out and plucking a few coarse hairs from just behind Grim's ears. *"Licking your balls doesn't count,"* I said, and I dropped the hairs into my coat pocket and strolled into the restaurant, leaving Grim outside to wait for me like a good boy.

The hours on a sign by the door indicated that the restaurant had only just opened, but I could've guessed that without the posting. I knew this ambiance all too well—the empty dining room, the unlit candles on each table, the vacant host stand. They clearly didn't expect anyone to come in for another hour or so, and why would they? I suspected that even in Eastwind, people weren't looking for greasy pizza and pasta before they'd even had their second cup of coffee. I'd only ever done that while I was in culinary school, and even then, it was cold pizza, and that's a different food entirely, far as I'm concerned.

I peeked into the dining area. A gorgeous man stood

behind the bar at the far wall, cleaning wine glasses. Except, he didn't use his hands for it.

He had an entire assembly line going in midair, wiping each glass clean of any smudges with a rag before it levitated to its proper place on a shelf or hung upside down by its foot in the wooden racks above the bar. All the bartender did was wave a thick wooden wand around, and the rest went off without a hitch.

Was I *that* kind of witch? Man, I sure hoped so. Housework was my least favorite activity in the world. If I could do it all with a simple flick of the wrist, I was all-in on the witch thing.

"Excuse me," I said, slightly worried that if I interrupted him all the fragile stemware would go crashing to the tiled floor. But that didn't happen. It froze in midair as he glanced over at me. Holy smokes, was he good looking! Where Tanner was gorgeous, this man was stunning. Like, steal-the-air-from-your-lungs hot. There was something alarming about him, like he was able to size me up in a single glance. It felt like he was undressing me with his eyes.

And I was very okay with that.

"Sit anywhere you like," he said, brushing me off, "and a server will be right with you."

Okay, so he wasn't undressing me with his eyes. That was just how he looked at everyone.

I found a seat in the corner and had only just settled when a tiny girl fluttered up to me—actually fluttered. Like the merchant at the berry cart, this girl was a fairy. I thought about what Grim said regarding fairies tampering with food, and I wasn't sure I wanted her as my server. But I decided to move forward with my plan.

"Hi there," she said brightly. "I'm Trinity, and I'll be your server today." As she continued the introduction, I smiled along, letting her finish her rehearsed greeting. Then I ordered the lasagna, because who doesn't love lasagna, and sat back, expecting it to be a while before the food arrived. They probably hadn't unpacked all the necessary ingredients yet, and the stove was probably still heating—

Oh right. Magic.

Two minutes later, Trinity fluttered out again with a steaming plate of lasagna. I thanked her and looked down regrettably at the food, knowing what I was about to do. Somewhere, people were starving, and here I was about to waste an entire entree.

Or wait, were there starving people in Eastwind? It was a small enough town that certainly no one was left on the fringes, right?

Sure. I'd take that.

Grim might be hungry, but I could deal with that later.

Once Trinity was out of sight, I slipped Grim's loose hairs from my pocket, the ones I'd pulled off him just a few minutes before, and, when I was sure hot bartender wasn't looking, slipped them in between the layers of the lasagna.

By the time I was able to flag down Trinity again, I'd managed most of my guilt about what I'd done and was able to fake an apologetic but displeased grimace. "Sorry, there's, um, hair in my food," I said.

What I'd expected was the reaction I'd given patrons over my many years in the service industry when they complained about their meal: a sympathetic frown, eyebrows pinched together, a little gasp at the outrage of it all, and then an empty apology and an offer to "see what I could do."

But what I received from Trinity was far worse.

"Oh my stars!" she said, cupping her hands over her mouth in horror and shaking her head slowly. Had I misspoken? Had I accidentally said, "Your grandmother has been mauled to death by a werewolf" instead of mentioning a few hairs in my lasagna? Judging by her reaction, it seemed likely.

Her wings stopped their rapid beating and she dropped out of the air, landing on her feet. I had to lean forward to see her over the tabletop.

"I have no idea how that happened!" she exclaimed. "The food is magically prepared especially to avoid contamination!"

Oops. Was hair in the food not a common thing here? I'd made an assumption, and now that I thought about it, if I had magic available to me, making sure no hair ever got in food would be toward the top of my list of things to use said magic to accomplish. Well done, Eastwind.

But that did leave me feeling especially guilty. My little trick might cause a total overhaul in their magical process, and all for nothing.

"It's fine, it's fine," I said, trying to comfort her. "How about you just go grab the manager and I'll talk it over with her?" This, of course, had been my plan all along. Except without Trinity's meltdown.

Horror washed over her face. "Are you going to tell on me? Please, please, miss, I'll do anything. Just don't tell Jane about this." She hopped back up into the air to get on eye level with me and whispered, "I'll do *anything*."

Whoa. I didn't like the way she'd said "anything" like it was actually carte blanche. Poor girl. Good thing she'd said it to me and not some horny man who might take full advantage of the offer.

So I improvised a little. The plan had been to plant the hair then ask to speak with a manager, whereupon Jane would be called over and I could pry about Bruce without being obvious that it was what I was doing. I didn't think it would help me get to the bottom of his murder if the prime suspect (only suspect at this point) knew what I was up to.

But my new approach would work just the same.

"I'm not going to tell Jane about this," I said, shushing her as calmingly as I could. When I glanced up, the sexy bartender was glaring at me. I shrugged lightly, hoping he'd take that to mean I wasn't responsible for the fact that the fairy was now ... crying?

Oh, come on.

"Sh-sh-shh... Trinity, listen." I'd managed my fair share of random server meltdowns, which was the situation in which I now found myself. Usually, I'd wait the thing out, provide enough sympathy for them to feel heard but not enough that it encouraged them to keep crying. Then I'd go kick out the customer who'd spurred the situation or fire the floor manager who'd created an environment that left servers so on edge.

Except I was the customer who'd made her cry. I hadn't meant to, but my intentions counted for jack squat. After all, I hadn't meant to crash my car into a tree, die, and end up in this town, trying to solve the murder of a werewolf.

Nope, couldn't think about all that right now.

"Don't worry, I won't speak to Jane about the hair. Hey, I have an idea! Why don't you bring her out here and I'll let her know how wonderful of service I've received. I won't mention anything about the hair. In fact,"—I pulled open the lasagna and pulled out three Grim hairs from it, wiping them on a napkin—"no one else needs to know."

I was pretty sure I'd shoved four hairs in there, so I made a quick note to self to go back for the last one before devouring the meal later. (The smells had my appetite roaring like a ... werelion? Did those exist?)

"You promise you won't tell her about the hair?"

"Pinkie swear."

She smiled and held out her pinkie, and I was immediately relieved that they had pinkie swearing here ... though admittedly I was confused about how it, of all things, made it from my world to Eastwind. Cars? Nope. But pinkie swearing? That's a big affirmative.

Once the pact was official, she flitted to the back, and I scooped a bite of the lasagna into my mouth, careful to avoid the section where the rogue hair might still be lodged.

Oh. My. God.

I took another bite.

Yep. Even after the second bite, I was sure this was the best lasagna I'd ever had. How did everything in Eastwind taste better than sex felt?

I paused in forking the third bite into my mouth when a beautiful woman with gorgeous cocoa skin glided out of the kitchen and toward my table.

Was this Jane Saxon? Bruce wasn't too hard on the eyes, but Jane was in an entirely different league. She was fierce, and her power flowed off of her in shockwaves with every step she took. I understood why Trinity was wary of her.

Oh, and she was a werewolf and could probably tear anyone in this restaurant to shreds if she wanted. Let's not forget that.

"Can I help you?" she asked. It sounded more like a challenge, as if the only obvious answer would be, "No, everything's great. I need nothing from you."

But I was here to solve her ex-husband's murder so he would leave me alone.

And, I guess, because it was the right thing to do. Eh, whatever.

There was no doubt in my mind, looking at Jane standing only a few feet from me, that she had the strength to take a man out with a frying pan. But would she?

"I'm new to town," I said, ignoring the slight arching of her eyebrow, "and a new friend recommended this place. I've spent my life working in restaurants, too, so I just wanted to let you know how incredible the food is."

When her shoulders softened, I knew I was making progress, so I continued. "If this town is anything like every other town, you only ever hear about the food when there's something wrong with it."

Her tense demeanor cracked. Grinning, she said, "In that respect, yes, Eastwind is like every other town."

Her smile was magic. I guess around here it could have literally been magic, but I mean it more in the figurative sense. Jane with a smile was *way* out of Bruce's league. I wondered why they divorced. Asking right then, though, likely wouldn't be the soft touch I needed to keep Jane open and friendly.

"My name's Nora," I said. "I, um, I don't know many people in town. If you're not too busy, would you want to have a seat?"

She looked around the empty restaurant and frowned. "I don't know ... we're awfully swamped around here." When her eyes returned to mine, we both chuckled and she sat.

Jane was incredibly likable once I got past the intimidation factor. Sure, she was the kind of woman whose bad side one should avoid getting on at all costs. But I've had people say that about me, before, so I didn't hold much stock in it. Something about women with boundaries and no time for BS is a little bit terrifying to the world.

I hoped Jane wasn't the murderer. My purpose of the visit suddenly changed from a neutral intelligence-gathering trip to an attempt to exonerate her from suspicion and cross her off the list of possible suspects.

And make her my friend.

Does that sound needy?

Then I guess I was needy. In my defense, if I was going to be stuck in Eastwind for the rest of my life, it made sense to find people I liked here. I couldn't rely entirely on Tanner the gorgeous waiter, Ruby the strange old psychic, and Grim the clinically depressed hound to satisfy my basic social needs.

"So," started Jane, "where did you come from?"

"Earth."

Jane bit her lip, holding back smile mercifully. "Right. But like, *where* on earth?"

Oh. Shoot. "Texas. Are you familiar with my world?"

She nodded. "I may look like I'm in my twenties, but I'm no spring pup here. We don't have people come in from your world often, but they come often enough, and when they do, guess where they go for a taste of home."

I nodded. "Ah, that makes sense. Who doesn't love Italian food?"

"Exactly. And our cuisine is second only to the home cooking over at—" When she cut herself off, my attention sharpened.

"Medium Rare?" I supplied.

She nodded. "Yes." Her eyes narrowed at me. "You know already. About me and Bruce."

"Rumors travel fast," I said apologetically.

She nodded somberly and flattened out a wrinkle in the tablecloth. "True, true. I didn't do it, you know."

"Didn't do what?"

"Mur— I would never hurt Bruce."

"I heard you two argued quite a bit."

Her shoulders tensed. "Have you ever argued with someone, Nora?"

I nodded.

"And did you then murder them?" she asked.

"Of course not," I said, sitting up straight.

"Then you know one doesn't necessarily lead to the other. Sure, Bruce and I argued. Sometimes we said horrible, unforgivable things to each other when our wolf-selves got the best of us. But sometimes that happens when people love each other. It's messy."

"But the arguing continued after you were divorced. Was it still out of love then?"

She swallowed hard and her bottom lip quivered.

"For me it was." I almost couldn't hear her, she spoke so quietly, and my heart broke for her.

She still loved him. She probably loved him more than I'd ever loved a man, and they'd divorced, and now he was dead. All hope of reconciliation was gone.

"I'm sorry," I said.

Sniffing sharply, she pulled herself together in a hurry, and the momentary glimpse of utter devastation vanished. "I'd bet money that hussy he was with had something to do with his death. I don't have anything against young, beautiful women, but"—she leaned forward conspiratorially—"you ever meet someone that's just a little *too* pretty? Just a little *too* flawless?" She leaned back again. "Anyone who puts that much time into their appearance is hiding something dark, in my opinion."

Half of me cringed at Jane's typical woman-hating-prettier-woman behavior.

And the other half of me knew *exactly* what she was saying. And agreed wholeheartedly.

"He was dating someone?" I asked, feeling slightly annoyed at Bruce's taciturn nature. If he wanted me to solve his murder, he should've been way more forthcoming with me instead of just pointing fingers at poor Jane.

Ah, right. This was exactly what Ruby was talking about. You couldn't trust the victim to be unbiased.

"Yeah. Some blonde Bimbo," said Jane. "I think her name is Fancy or... Tancy? Oh!" She snapped her fingers. "Tandy. That was it. She works over at Echo's Salon. She's some kind of ... I don't actually know what she is. Maybe a nymph? My friend Hyacinth works at Echo's, too, and says she's never met a worse person in her life. Of course, Tandy *seems* sweet, but we all know that the girls who never say mean things spend all their free time plotting mean things. Gotta blow off the steam somehow. Honesty is a virtue, after all. Holding it all in isn't healthy. Blunt is best, in my opinion."

"I can tell," I said.

For a moment, Jane's eyes widened and she looked upset, then the flash was gone, and she grinned mischievously. "Oh, I like you." She wagged a finger at me. "Good luck with this town, though. It's jam-packed full of people who are so desperate for everything to be perfect that they let things fester. I haven't lived anywhere else, but I've traveled to connecting lands and I talk to a lot of people, so I feel pretty safe saying the murder rate is higher in Eastwind than just about anywhere else. Things can only bubble under the surface for so long before they boil over. And when you're dealing with a whole mixing pot of creatures, things draw to a head sooner than later."

"Thanks for the warning," I said.

"Ah, well, don't worry too much about it," she said. "I assume you're a witch, right?"

"Apparently so."

"People try not to mess with witches around here. They'll bring the full weight of the Coven down on their head if they do. That's not to say witches don't end up dead now and again. But if you stay out of trouble, you'll be fine." Though she grinned comfortingly, I did not, in fact, feel comforted.

"Good to know. I guess."

"Your food is getting cold," she said, nodding down at my lasagna.

"Could I get a check and a to-go box?" I asked. "I just remembered that my dog is waiting outside."

She stood from the table, looking at me sideways. "This one's on me. And I thought witches were supposed to have cats."

And I thought witches weren't real, but things change. "I've always had a problem doing what everyone else does."

Jane fetched (is that an offensive verb for a werewolf?) me a to-go box and bag, and asked me to come by anytime I liked for fifty percent off my meal since I was new ... but mostly because she liked me. I wouldn't say no to that.

But for now, I had to get a move on. I hadn't been to a salon in, oh, seven years? I was way overdue for a visit.

Chapter Seven

I didn't expect to find Tandy at Echo's Salon. After all, her boyfriend was murdered the day before. For someone like Jane, putting on a brave face and pushing forward seemed almost a compulsion, but from the little I knew of Tandy (or women like her), she didn't seem cut from the same durable cloth.

Yet there she was.

I knew it was her the moment I laid eyes on her through the large salon window facing out onto a main road a few blocks away from the emporium. Echo's Salon was nestled among shops for Eastwind's wealthier inhabitants. On one side of the salon was a jeweler and on the other a clothing boutique shop with magicked mannequins in long, sleek robes switching from one posh pose to another in the storefront window.

I paused, peering into the salon. All the stylists were beautiful, but I could pick out which one was Tandy right away. She shined like a star among them. Her silver-blonde hair flowed down to her waist in robust waves, and her complexion was smooth and luminous. As for her body, it reminded me of a Barbie. Actually, *she* reminded me of a Barbie, one of the older ones from the Fifties with the squinty eyes.

I never liked Barbies. For one, they were always blonde, curvy, long-legged. My hair had been the same medium brown since the day I was born, straight on one side, not quite straight on the other. And no one would ever describe me as curvy. In fact, I nearly threw myself a party when I last went to buy a bra and found I was actually a B-cup rather than an A-cup. Barbies had never left me feeling good about myself growing up, and they'd made me feel even worse when I saw the way my childhood best friend Shonda's face sagged every time there was no Barbie with the same cocoa skin she had. And the few times we'd spotted one in the toy store, she'd examined the Barbie's long, slick hair, and then touched her own, which was coarse and roamed free in every direction.

Tandy was a Barbie incarnate, not only in looks but in the way she made me feel when I looked at her. I thought back to Jane, then to Shonda, both beautiful women who were made to feel bad by the mere existence of Barbies.

And then I felt guilty. I mean, *seriously* guilty. It wasn't Tandy's fault she looked that way. Sure, she must have spent a lot of time on her appearance, but that just went to show the pressure even beautiful women felt to be flawless and pleasant for men to gaze upon.

I needed to retract the claws and give Tandy a fair chance.

"Here," I said to Grim as I opened the take-out bag and box and set it on the ground. "For your troubles."

"You think I need your handouts? Please ..." But not a second later, he was snout-deep in lukewarm lasagna.

Every chair in the salon was occupied when I entered. The stylists and clients chattered passionately among each other.

I planted my feet in shock, once I saw the way things worked here. What kind of beings were these? Jane had mentioned something about nymphs, but I didn't know much about those.

One stylist was in charge of the hair washing process for each client. He approached the chair where a slender, raven-haired woman waited, and then he waved an open palm around her head until water soaked the hair from root to tip. "There you go, love," he said, before crossing the salon to another stylist who flagged him down.

Meanwhile, a short and plump woman, whose hair swirled around her like she was caught in the world's gentlest tornado, approached the client nearest to me, whose stylist had just completed the last snip of her cut. The plump woman held a flat palm on each side of the client's wet hair, and as she did so, her hair fell limp and the client's began to whip around in a breeze until it was not only dry but styled in silky-smooth waves. As soon as the plump woman removed her hands, her own hair took to the breeze again.

"You must be new here," said a voice from behind the reception desk. I turned to see a mousy young man leaning back in his chair and filing his nails. "We don't get many new people, but the look is the same every time. Did you want to make an appointment?"

"Please. With Tandy."

He nodded and leaned toward me, so I bent forward to meet him halfway. "Poor thing." He spoke it like a whisper but with enough volume to be easily overheard by the clients closest to the desk. "Her boyfriend was just murdered. *Yesterday.*" He leaned back, eyes wide, nodding slowly.

"You don't say."

Jane wasn't kidding about this place being a gossip hub. He'd offered up that bit without any prompting. Maybe it'd be easier than I'd hoped to mine some useful information about Bruce's murder from Echo's Salon.

And if I could get a nice hairstyle, even better. I couldn't remember the last time I made myself an appointment at a salon. I'd had the money but never the time.

"I'm surprised she's here today," I said to the receptionist. "I'd definitely call in sick if my boyfriend were murdered the day before."

He nodded slowly but emphatically and mouthed, *me too*, then he leaned forward again, unable to stem the flow of gossip. "They were so in love. You should have seen the two of them together. Always touching inappropriately in public. It used to drive Echo insane, but I always thought it was kind of hot to watch."

Ew. I hurriedly steered the conversation to less creepy, voyeuristic waters. "Who's Echo?"

"Who's Echo?" he echoed. "Ha! Only the owner of this fine establishment. Echo Chambers is *easily* the most stylish person in all of Eastwind. Without him, this town wouldn't be half as fabulous as it is."

"Well, then thank god for him," I said, and the receptionist pressed his lips together tightly and nodded without catching the slightest whiff of my sarcasm.

"Ladavian," came a sweet singsong voice from just behind me. I turned to find Tandy floating over. Not literally floating, I should specify that, I guess. But her gait was so smooth, it was like watching water walk. "Help this lovely woman check out, please."

Behind her followed a sheepish middle-age woman, whose dark hair was now far too youthful and silky for her face.

As Ladavian did so, Tandy turned to me and smiled. "I've never seen you before. You must be Nora."

"Word travels fast in this town."

She laughed airily. "And faster in Echo's. I know too much about people around here, honestly." She paused, and her eyes looked me up and down, assessing me. "Are you here for a cut?" She reached forward and pinched a lock of my hair between two fingers, pulling down to the ends to inspect them. "I could snip off these dead ends for you and it would make all the difference."

"Um, thanks," I said, recognizing a backhanded compliment when it smacked me in the face, "but I just want a blowout today. Maybe tomorrow I'll come back for a trim."

"Ah," she said, sounding disappointed. But then she perked up again quickly. "Right this way!"

She led me over to an empty chair in a row of four and wrapped a towel around my shoulders, addressing me in the mirror. "Can I get you something to drink? A fizz rejuvenator or a citrus blast?"

"I'm not sure what those are," I said, looking around for signs of other customers drinking them.

She beamed, her squinty eyes two dark slits of long lashes. "Oh, well, in that case, you *have* to try the citrus blast. It tastes like fresh orange juice but replenishes whatever minerals you lack. It'll do wonders to help with these." She brushed the tip of her finger over bags under my eyes.

I decided against sharply informing her that the bags were caused by hopping worlds, witnessing a murder, and then being harangued by a ghost all night (the ghost of her dead boyfriend, no less) rather than an ongoing nutrient deficiency.

Which reminded me why I was there. Not the nutrient deficiency, but the ghost. The murder. "Citrus blast sounds great," I said. She grabbed one from a tray at the end of the row and handed it to me. It was served in a spherical glass bubble with an open top out of which stuck a glass straw. Points for presentation.

"If you want a wash, we need Augustus." She motioned at the hair washer to work his magic, which he did quickly and dispassionately without a single word of greeting to me.

Once he was done, he hurried off again, except he went to the front desk to whisper conspiratorially with Ladavian since there wasn't currently another stylist in need of his services.

"You were there, weren't you?" Tandy said, leaning forward as I sipped my citrus blast (which was delicious). She massaged sweet earthy oils into my wet scalp.

"Where?" I asked.

"At Medium Rare, when Bruce was murdered."

I swallowed the drink hard. This was why I was here, wasn't it? Not for the scalp massage, not for the citrus blast.

"Yes, I was. You knew him?"

Her nostrils flared gently and she made a weird chirping sound in her throat. "Yes," she breathed. "We were in love."

"I'm so sorry," I replied, pretending this was new information to me.

"I just got the news this morning. I almost didn't come into work." She bit her bottom lip as it began to quiver.

"I'm surprised you did," I said, trying to sound sympathetic rather than suspicious.

"I guess I'm still in shock," she said. "It doesn't seem real that Bruce was here yesterday and gone today. It just —" Her voice cracked. "I decided that I'd rather be here, surrounded by my friends than at home by myself. The thought of spending the day alone in my bed, the same one where Bruce and I made such passionate love day after day sounded like an especially cruel form of torture."

While I could've done without the visual of this young, breathtakingly beautiful blonde tangled up in bed with the bulky Bruce "hairy forearms" Saxon, her story did start to make sense.

I wouldn't want to be alone if the love of my life was murdered. I would want to be wherever made me happiest.

I'd been unfair in my judgment of Tandy. Everyone

mourns differently, and she shouldn't have to sit at home and tough it out if she had a way to take her mind off of it. The sadness would always be there for her to come back to.

I'd learned that hard lesson when my parents were killed. The first year afterward was torture, but I'd always felt guilty about finding respite from the despair, so I'd forced myself to feel the pain, never allowing much-needed breaks.

I wished I'd taken Tandy's route, now that I thought about it. In the end, the pain never amounted to anything worthwhile. And it never brought them back.

"I'm so sorry, Tandy." I'd already said it, but I figured saying it a second time wouldn't hurt. I meant it more this time anyway.

She nodded somberly. "Thanks." Then, after a deep intake of air, she leaned forward and said, "Do you like your hair blown forward toward your face or backward to show off your cheekbones?"

"I don't think I have a preference. I just tuck it behind my ears either way."

"Ah. Okay." She sounded disappointed. "We'll blow it forward. Laurel!"

The windy woman hurried over and Tandy relayed the directions to her. Laurel made quick work of my hair and I was surprised by how much of a change a simple, thoughtful blow-dry could improve in my entire appearance.

"How do you like it?" Tandy asked, removing the towel around my neck.

"It's great. Thank you."

She beamed modestly. "Oh, please. It's your gorgeous

hair. We just bring out its full potential. And the citrus blast doesn't hurt either." She winked.

"Can I ask you something?"

She nodded.

"I hate to bring up a sore subject again, but did Bruce have any enemies that you know of?"

Her face darkened slightly and she leaned forward to avoid being overheard. "I've been thinking about this, too. I keep coming back to Ansel."

"Ansel?"

"Ansel Fontaine. Jane Saxon's boyfriend."

"Why would he want to hurt Bruce?"

"Well, because everyone knows Jane wasn't over Bruce, and Ansel is a total puppy dog for her. Or, I guess a total cub for her, since he's a werebear. I heard he wants to propose but hasn't because she's still so hung up on Bruce. I guess she thought they might get back together and didn't want to commit fully to Ansel while that was still a possibility. Poor Jane. And Ansel. And Bruce." She sighed. "It's just a bad situation all around, but Bruce being out of the picture benefits Ansel the most, since Jane will have to give up her foolish hope. Plus, if you meet Ansel, you'll realize that, while he might be all cute and cuddly to Jane, the rest of Eastwind steers clear of him. He has quite a temper."

"Thanks for the heads up," I said. "I'll keep that in mind." A beautiful bit of harp music started playing in the salon. I wondered briefly if it'd always been playing and I hadn't noticed it or if it had just started. The beauty of it almost brought me to tears.

Wait, music was about to bring me to tears? Was it

that time of the month already? I thought I still had a solid two weeks.

"Are you going to talk with him?" she asked, narrowing her eyes at me. Then something seemed to click. "Oh! Wait! Are you trying to solve the murder?"

I shrugged. "Yes, I guess so."

She leaned close again and whispered, "Is that so Deputy Manchester doesn't arrest you? I heard you were a suspect." She grimaced sympathetically, then added, "I don't think you did it, though. Why would you? Also, I'm a great judge of character. I may not be a witch like you"—how did everyone know I was a witch just by looking at me?—"but I have pretty good intuition about who's pure of heart and who's got a guilty conscience."

"That's a good skill to have," I said.

"Do you like it?" she asked.

"Like what?"

"The music. Is it to your liking?"

"Oh. Yes. I was just noticing it. Between us, it almost brought me to tears just a second ago."

"Yes, it used to be one of my favorite pieces. I'm afraid it's starting to grate after this many listens, though. Glad you can enjoy it." She rotated the chair, signaling that it was time for me to go, and I followed her over to the reception desk. "Ladavian, since Nora's new to town, we're going to make her feel welcome. This one's on me."

I looked quickly from Ladavian to Tandy. "Huh? No, you don't need to. I have money."

She placed a gentle hand on my shoulder to silence me, and I stared into her gorgeous eyes, all bitterness about how much prettier she was than me disappearing under the barrage of admiration for her appearance.

"Please, Nora. I need to do something nice for someone else today."

That I understood. Sometimes grief can only be assuaged through kind acts for others. "Okay. I'm coming back to see you, though, and then you'll have to take my money. Deal?"

Beaming, she reached forward and ran her fingers through my hair where it hung in front of my shoulders, giving it a little extra body. "Deal. Just do me one favor, will you?"

"Of course."

"Go speak with Ansel right away. He works out at Whirligig's Garden Center. Tall, muscular black guy. Not too hard on the eyes, if I do say so. If you're going to solve Bruce's murder, you have to speak with Ansel. I promise you Deputy Manchester won't even think of it. Heck, he hasn't even interviewed *me* yet. It seems like any proper officer of the law would go to the lover first thing." She sighed. "I'm glad you're here, Nora."

The harp music crescendoed in the background, and I surprised myself when I said, truthfully, "Me too."

She walked with me to the front door, and when Grim stood up and loped over, Tandy gasped. "Is he yours?"

"Um, sort of."

"I bet your familiar hates that," she said.

"He, um ... he *is* my familiar."

She turned quickly to stare at me. "Your familiar is a dog?"

I shrugged. "Yeah. Looks like it."

"Huh." She stared at Grim. "Huh."

He kept his distance from us, eying me judgmentally.

"*You done with your girl's day out? Can we get back to solving the murder?*"

I shot him a sharp look.

"You know," Tandy said, "I'm actually quite talented with animals. I'd be happy to give him a wash and trim for you. I should have time for it tomorrow."

"Yes," I said enthusiastically. "That would be *wonderful*, Tandy. I think Grim would really enjoy that."

"*If that fairy thing lays a hand on me, I will aggressively mark everything in that salon. You will not believe how much pee I have in the tank until you see it in action.*"

Tandy crouched down, holding a hand out to Grim. "Come here, boy. Let me get a look at those mats."

Grim backed up two steps.

"He's a little shy," I explained. "He was the runt of the litter and always got picked on. Now he trusts no one. Except me. Poor damaged soul."

"*I hope you're enjoying this,*" Grim said. "*Because I will find a way to get back at you.*"

"What's that?" I asked him, then I turned to Tandy. "He asked if you have any lavender scented shampoo. It's his favorite scent."

"Of course! I'll make sure to have it ready for tomorrow."

"Sounds great. See you then."

I waved goodbye to Tandy and turned my back to Echo's. "*Okay, Grim, where's Whirligig's Garden Center?*"

"*You just expect me to help you now?*"

"*Oh come on, I was just having a little fun. I wouldn't let her bathe you in lavender.*"

"*Oh really?*"

"*Yeah, I enjoy the scent of rosemary far more. I'd have her bathe you in that.*"

"*Oh, you're SO funny,*" he said sarcastically, padding ahead of me. "*Garden center this way, Princess Funnypants.*"

Chapter Eight

Turned out, Grim was more passive-aggressive than any dog I'd ever met.

He got us to the garden center, yes, but only after we'd circled by the same few spots in town multiple times. My feet were killing me, and having only eaten a few bites of lasagna since breakfast, my stomach growled fiercely by the time we reached the vine-covered archways leading into the garden center.

The narrow cobblestone side street opened at the end of two stone buildings, and what lay beyond was almost unbelievable.

This was either Whirligig's Garden Center or simply the Garden of Eden. I would have put my money on the latter. I wondered if crossing into the garden center would actually put me in an entirely different world.

A tall stone wall stretched out in either direction, facing off against the stone and brick of downtown Eastwind, but it was almost impossible to see any of the fence since it was so thickly covered in vines and violet blossoms.

Downtown Eastwind looked like it was pulled from some fairy tale, but the garden center was a step above. I'd never seen such lushness. The trees were covered in moss that was covered in moss. It was like someone had painted a canvas bright green and then added splatters of vivid color here and there just to prove that whatever you *thought* you knew about plants was all wrong.

I stood at the entrance, which was a tunnel of stone archways covered in vines that stretched from one arch to the next, creating a cozy canopy.

"Why are we here?" Grim asked.

I'd forgotten that he wasn't in on the conversation with Tandy. *"We need to talk to Ansel Fontaine."*

"Ansel as in werebear Ansel?"

"Yes."

Grim's tail wagged. *"He runs with me in the Deadwoods sometimes in bear form. Werebears can be real tools, but Ansel is alright."*

"Tandy said he has a temper."

Grim bobbed his large head. *"Oh yeah. No doubt about it. I've seen him level a tree when he was angry."*

"Right. Okay. Well, I'll try not to set him off."

I followed as Grim padded forward beneath the archways. *"Nah,"* he said. *"He'd never hurt a woman."*

"Glad to hear it. But it wasn't a woman who was murdered last night."

"You think he murdered Bruce?"

"I don't think anything just yet. Tandy thinks it's a possibility."

"Tandy also thought I would let her bathe me in

lavender, so maybe she doesn't know anything about anything."

Grim ran ahead to greet Ansel when he spotted him.

Tandy wasn't joking when she said Ansel was easy on the eyes. It probably helped that he had his shirt off and sweat glistened on him like the dew in a honeysuckle, just waiting to be licked off.

Small saplings surrounded Ansel on three sides and by the looks of it, he was transplanting them to larger pots. He'd just set one, roots heavy with clotted mud, into an oversized pot when Grim trotted over.

"Hey, man!" Ansel said when he spotted Grim. "What brings you out of the Deadwoods?" He didn't expect an answer, which was good because Grim didn't give him one. Instead, the dog sat in front of him and offered a paw, which Ansel grabbed. They shook.

"Ansel Fontaine?" I said as I approached.

He looked up at me, his easygoing demeanor shifting to suspicion. "Yes?"

"Hi. I'm Nora Ashcroft. I'm, um, new in town." Shoot. I didn't know where to go from there. I couldn't just start questioning him. He didn't know who I was, and he had a temper. If he was the one who'd killed Bruce, that was a recipe for disaster.

So instead, I took a different tack.

"You know Grim?"

Ansel arched an eyebrow at me. "Who?"

"Oh. Him." I pointed.

"Ah. I didn't know he had a name. But I guess that one makes sense. Yeah, he and I go back." He looked me up and down. "I'm curious how you got him to come out of the woods and into so-called civilized society."

"He didn't have much of a choice," I said. "He's my familiar."

For a moment, Ansel stared blankly at me. Then he threw his head back and laughed.

"This is so embarrassing," Grim groaned, tucking his tail between his legs.

"My man!" Ansel said, finally able to speak again. "I never thought I'd see the day when you became domesticated."

"Tell him I'm not domesticated."

"He's not really domesticated," I said. "And neither of us is particularly happy about the match, if I'm being honest."

Ansel wiped a tear from his eyes. "Woo, man. I needed that. And I've never heard of a canine familiar. Well, no wait, doesn't Ruby have one?"

I nodded. "Clifford."

"Yeah." His eyes narrowed. "Are you like her?"

"Honestly, I'm not sure yet. I just got here. I didn't even know I was a witch until this morning."

He jerked his head back. "Oh, dang. That's heavy."

"Agreed."

"Where are you staying?"

"Ruby's."

"Ahh ..." He narrowed his eyes thoughtfully, and I could tell he was putting the pieces together. New witch in town. Dog familiar. Staying with Ruby. Finding him the day after a murder occurred.

"I take it you didn't come out here to buy plants," he said.

"Not today."

"You're here about Saxon's murder."

I nodded.

"I guess Ruby really is in retirement, now." He sighed. "I won't lie to you. I hated Bruce. The way he treated Jane"—the muscles in his forearms flexed as he clenched his gloved hands into fists—"it wasn't right. No one should treat another person that way. He was always flaunting his other women in front of her, too."

"Yeah, I'm starting to get the idea Bruce had a weakness for women."

"You could say that again. And for reasons far beyond my comprehension, they had a weakness for him."

"Is that why he and Jane divorced?"

He hesitated, cringing slightly. Then the tight cords of his muscular arms released. "Basically. She suspected he was cheating on her. Took a while for her to come to that conclusion, though. She'd just assumed Bruce was a flirt, nothing more. But then things started piling up. He'd say he was one place, then change his story a few days later. A handful of his admirers started acting just a little too familiar when they came into Medium Rare. And Jane had to sit there and watch it all happen. Finally, she got sick of it. She accused him of being unfaithful and said she wanted a divorce. He called her bluff and agreed to it, though he said he hadn't been cheating. Tried to turn it on her, in the end. He said he couldn't be with a woman who didn't trust him to be faithful. That jerk played the victim." Shaking his head, he pressed his lips together. There was sheer rage in his eyes. It was lucky Bruce was dead and not standing there in the garden center with us, or Ansel might've killed him right in front of me.

"But I knew," Ansel went on. "Heck, the whole town

knew. It wasn't a week after the divorce was finalized that he started running around with Tandy, bringing her everywhere, showing her off. He let up on the display for a while, and I thought he'd move on and so would Jane, but just last week, he brought Tandy into Franco's Pizza on a date, stoked the pain and bitterness inside Jane all over again."

"Oh god, that's awful." I felt the primal female impulse to invite Jane to a hard-core ladies wine night. Pjs, snack food, chocolate, whatever Eastwind's equivalent of Netflix was, lots of ranting—the whole shebang.

"I'll be honest with you," Ansel added. "I spent all last week fantasizing about murdering Bruce."

That sure yanked me from my indulgent wine-night reverie. "Come again?"

"Jane couldn't let it go. Mostly because he wouldn't let her let it go. Every time she started to really get over him, he'd find a way to remind her that he was fine without her. She may have initiated the divorce, but it was like he was set on rubbing her face in it every chance he could." He stepped toward me, and I could feel the rage radiating from him like heat waves. "I love that woman more than anything in this world, and I know she loves me, but I'd never get to be with her the way I wanted so long as Bruce was around, pulling her back in every time she was about to move on."

I couldn't breathe. Was this a confession? It sure sounded like a confession.

"I dreamed about it," he said. "Fantasized about all the ways I could murder him and get away with it. Maybe dump his body somewhere beyond the Outskirts in the Deadwoods, so by the time it was found, it'd already be picked clean. There were days when I'd shift into my bear and maul a tree, imagining it was Bruce." He took a step back. "It made me feel better, but it never helped Jane." He sighed. "In the end, I could never do it, because she still loved him, as tainted as it was. Killing Bruce would've felt incredible, but it would've hurt the woman I loved. I couldn't do that.

"I didn't murder him, but part of me wishes I had." He chuckled mirthlessly and motioned to some bright yellow blossoms beside him. "Let me know when you figure out who did it, and I'll send them some flowers."

My heart was still racing, and I looked down at Grim, who wagged his tail slowly. *"See? What's not to love about this guy?"*

At least one of us found murderous rage endearing.

"If you had to guess," I began, "who would your money be on for having done it?"

He shrugged. "Could be a lot of people. Bruce was well liked by the ladies, but not so much by the ladies' men. He could've stepped out of line with the wrong girl. Or maybe"—he paused, his eyes checking to make sure we were alone, "someone had something financial to gain from his death. Real estate in Eastwind ain't cheap, even on the Outskirts. Medium Rare does okay for itself. I know Jane used to be the beneficiary in the event of Bruce's death, but I assume he's changed that since the divorce."

"They didn't have any kids, though, right?"

"Thankfully, no."

"So who would it go to?"

He shrugged lightly, and the movement caused the

beads of sweat on his chest to catch the light ... and my attention.

Focus, Nora!

"My best guess would be Mr. Likable himself. Everybody leaves something to that kid in their will. It wouldn't surprise me if Bruce listed him as the sole beneficiary. Wouldn't be the first someone did that for everybody's favorite orphan."

"Um, forgive me for not knowing, but I *am* new here. Who exactly are you talking about?"

"Tanner. Tanner Culpepper."

"The gorge—um. The one that works at Medium Rare?"

He nodded. "Everybody loves that guy. I swear, every time someone turns up dead, he's listed in their will. After a few times, it starts to get just a little *too* suspicious for my liking. And everybody knows Tanner loves Medium Rare like it's his home. I'm not condemning him right off the bat, but I do think it's smart to check the will. If it's not Tanner, it's somebody, and that somebody could very well be your murderer."

"You don't sound like a fan of Tanner's," I said, trying not to give away how annoyed the thought made me.

Ansel held up his hands defensively. "I think he's great. Got no complaints here. I'm just saying, anyone who's that nice all the time is hiding something. He's just a little *too* nice, you know? If he's not working his butt off, he's running around town helping little old witches cross the street or rebuilding someone's house after a spell backfires or making personal house calls to his regulars if they don't show up for a few days. And he never asks for anything in return. Why would someone be that nice?"

He had a point. And it bore similarities to Jane's case against Tandy. Perhaps Jane and Ansel were a good match after all.

But I did like to believe that there were selfless people in the world. I just hadn't met many. Or any. "You got me there," I said. "I'll ask Bruce who he listed in his will, then I'll follow that trail."

He glanced at me sideways. "Hold up. Did you just say you'll ask Bruce? As in dead-guy-Bruce?"

"Uhh …" I looked to Grim for some help, but he had wandered a few feet away from the conversation and was rolling on his back in a fresh flowerbed. "No?"

Ansel was too sharp. "Makes sense. That's why you're here, huh? Not the first time Bruce won't stop pestering a beautiful woman who isn't interested in him. I don't know why I'd expect him to change just because he's dead."

I tried not to focus on the fact that he'd just called me beautiful.

"So, I guess he doesn't know who killed him, either?" Ansel added.

Since my jig was up, I decided to be honest. "No. He didn't see who it was."

"Sucks for you."

I chuckled. "Yeah. Yeah, it does."

"I'd better get back to work."

"Thanks for the chat."

He nodded once. "And do what I told you. Figure out who gets Medium Rare. That's what I'd do … if I could talk to dead guys."

I agreed and called Grim to follow me. But before

we'd made it ten feet, Ansel called after us, "Oh, and can you do me a favor?"

Everyone and their favors. "Sure," I said.

"Tell Bruce that ..."

I'll spare you the rest of the message since it wasn't anything good.

"Later, *Grim*," Ansel said teasingly. Grim waved a paw at him and led the way out of the garden center.

I needed to get back to Ruby True's place and have a word with old Bruce.

Chapter Nine

"You didn't have a strong feeling about any of them?" Ruby asked as she sat across the parlor table from me. She'd been kind enough to whip me up a hearty beef stew once I returned from Whirligig's. I was amazed how quickly she managed it. She may not have the same powers as most witches, but she definitely knew her way around a kitchen. And she seemed to have the same basic tastes as me.

Not the taste for fine dining; that was something I'd forced myself to develop. The stew was simple—beef stock, potatoes, carrots, onions, cabbage, and fresh garlic cloves with thick hunks of tender beef—but it filled me up in ways that extended beyond my basic appetite. It made me feel calm, secure, the way good home cooking should.

I needed to get this recipe.

Clifford, Ruby's familiar who was Grim's equal in size but had fiery red hair with a few grays in the mix, barked in his sleep from his place by the fire. I hadn't yet seen him in motion. It was almost like he appeared out of thin air, already snoozing. Maybe someday I could find time to get that much sleep.

But not anytime soon. I had pressing matters to attend to, now that I was starting to get my wits about me again as my wooden bowl progressed toward empty.

"I had strong feelings about them, but it was hard to separate the personal from the objective."

"Meaning?" Bruce said from his place floating just above a chair that Ruby had been kind enough to pull out for him at the parlor table. I wondered if he was at all embarrassed about his need for the charade of sitting when everyone could tell there was no actual physical contact between him and the chair.

"Meaning, I don't think it's Ansel, but I don't know if that's because Grim really likes him or because his honesty about how much he would have liked to murder you seemed a little too brazen for a killer.

"Then there's Tandy, who, no offense, Bruce, I immediately disliked. But that's probably more about me being petty toward someone that beautiful than anything related to your murder. And then I started to trust her the more we talked, but I'm not sure if that's because her reason for showing up at work rather than staying home made sense to me, or because she made my hair look so good for free." I held up a hand before anyone said a word. "I know, not one of my prouder admissions.

"And then there's Jane." I paused unsure what to say that would explain why I was sure she hadn't done it without betraying her.

"You can't tell me she didn't have it out for me," Bruce said. "The last time I went into Franco's Pizza, she nearly bit my head off. I mean, literally. She was starting to shift into her wolf, she was so angry. She told me she had half a mind to finish shifting and tear me to shreds."

I assumed this was the same visit Ansel had mentioned, but I needed to make sure. "The last time you went to Franco's Pizza, did you by any chance bring Tandy along?"

His translucent mouth opened, but no words came out.

Ruby didn't bother disguising her judgment as she arched two eyebrows, turning slightly in her seat to face him directly. "Well, isn't this interesting," she said, crossing her arms and leaning back to get a better look at him.

"What?" he said finally. "*She* was the one who asked *me* for the divorce! I don't get to date anyone after that?"

"Bruce," Ruby said coldly. "We don't have time for your nonsense. You know as well as anyone that you don't bring your new lover to your ex's place of work."

"But the lasagna's so good," he protested weakly. "I have to deprive myself of lasagna just because my ex-wife chose to work at the best restaurant in town? Besides Medium Rare, obviously," he added quickly.

"Yes," Ruby and I said at the same time. Then I added, "Sorry, but this is part of why divorce sucks."

He wasn't getting it, though, so I tried a new approach to hint without blatantly outing Jane. "Why do you think Jane might have been so angry about you bringing Tandy to dinner there?"

"Because she hates everything about me," Bruce said sulkily.

"Try again," I said.

He paused to think about it, then slowly said, "She was jealous?"

I nodded, indicating he should go on.

"But she has Ansel. She's moved on, too."

"Has she?" I asked.

"Hmm," he said. Then, "Hmm ... Yeah, I suppose that makes sense." He lowered his head, shaking it slowly. "I had no idea." He moved his ghastly hands up to his face. "What an idiot I've been."

I felt bad for the guy, but at the same time, for someone who seemed to be quite the ladies' man, he sure didn't understand ladies.

"I don't think Jane wanted you dead," I concluded. "But I need to know something, Bruce."

He lifted his head from his hands and said in a self-pitying voice. "Yes?"

"Who does Medium Rare go to, now that you're dead?"

He sat up straight. "Well, Tanner, of course."

Of course.

Shoot, Ansel might've been onto something.

"And does he know that?" I asked, hoping he did not. So long as Tanner was unaware, the will couldn't function as a motive.

Bruce considered it. "Well, I'm not sure. I'd only gotten around to changing it from Jane to Tanner last week. Things had been so busy around the diner that ... yeah, I don't think I mentioned it to him."

I exhaled with relief. "Then he can't be a suspect."

"I mean, he might've heard about it from someone else," Bruce added.

"Like who?"

He scrunched up his face, causing his appearance to swirl slightly with the movement. "Quinn Shaw was my estate attorney, so he was in charge of making the changes. I doubt he would take it upon himself to inform the beneficiaries, but there's a good chance he told his son, Seamus."

"Why would he tell his son?"

"Quinn's been trying to get Seamus into the family business for years. Unfortunately, Seamus has trouble with … well, with anything that requires responsibility. But Seamus likes his drink. I wouldn't put it past Seamus to tell Tanner I'd changed my will to leave Medium Rare to him. I've seen the two of them together down at Sheehan's Pub before. Could've happened there."

"I guess there's only one way to settle this," I said, my heart skipping a beat at the thought. "I'll head down to Medium Rare in the morning and have a chat with Tanner."

Chapter Ten

I hated how nervous I was, approaching Medium Rare the next day. And before you give me the benefit of the doubt, no, I wasn't nervous about talking to a possible murderer. I was nervous about seeing Tanner again for personal reasons. Namely, because I couldn't get him out of my mind.

My eyes locked onto him through the front windows before I ever set foot in the place. It was almost gravitational.

It wasn't until the front doorbell tinkled overhead and I entered the warm diner that my eyes also found the girl he was talking to at the counter.

I almost turned around and walked out.

She was way prettier than me, and in that girl-next-door way that guys go gaga over. She had curves, too. Her face was round and youthful in the way that invites open and friendly conversation with strangers. Meanwhile, I'd been described on more than one occasion as having a raging case of Resting Bitch Face, and not in a female werewolf sort of way.

It wasn't even a competition between the two of us. *Of course* Tanner would chase after a girl like that. They were two beautiful peas in a pod, and as I stood there like a frozen idiot, watching the two of them relate, I could tell just by her body language that she was probably as nice and friendly as he was. If this place had the typical high school scene, I'd put money on the two of them being homecoming king and queen. Probably uncontested, even.

Finally, Tanner unintentionally caught sight of me and his face lit up. "Nora! We were just talking about you! Come here." He waved me over exaggeratedly, and I pitched a smile on my face and approached like I wasn't totally concocting an entire life story for the two of them.

The girl turned on her stool to face me directly.

Shoot. Just looking at her put me at ease. This wasn't someone who would judge me; this was someone who would tell me to stop judging myself. Ugh. People like that were equal parts delightful and annoying.

"Nora, this is Zoe Clementine. She recently moved here from Avalon."

"Oh." That certainly changed things. At least the homecoming queen scenario was no longer a possibility. "Nice to meet—"

"Oh my god, I'm so happy to meet you!" Zoe said, interrupting me. "I've heard so many wonderful things about you from Tanner. And, truth be told, I've felt a little like an outsider since I got here, so it's nice to have someone else around who's not born in Eastwind."

"There are plenty of other people from Avalon who live in Eastwind," Tanner said.

She waved him off. "Oh, sure, but they're, like, *Avalonian* Avalonians. High fashion, refined taste, all that. They came here to bring Avalon to Eastwind. I came here to be in Eastwind as it is. This town is just so precious!"

Back home, Zoe was not the type of person I spent time with, but after just over a day in Eastwind, I was starting to wonder if the person I was back home was someone *I* would want to spend time with now.

"I gotta run," she said, grabbing a to-go box off the counter. "The animals can't feed themselves!" She turned to me. "It was great meeting you, Nora. We'll have to catch up sometime."

"Sounds good." For the record, I meant it.

Once she left, Tanner filled me in. "She's been running my grandmother's animal sanctuary since she passed away last summer."

"I'm sorry to hear about your grandmother, Tanner."

"It's fine. I mean, it's not fine. Everyone's pretty sure she left the sanctuary to me, but I don't know the first thing about taking care of all those animals. Zoe wanted a job, had experience with animals in Avalon, so we agreed that she'd be the unofficial owner until the dang last will and testament moves through probate in the Parchment Catacombs and we can know for sure who the sanctuary goes to."

"And how long does that take?"

"Oh, you know, four to four hundred weeks. Organization isn't a strong suit of the catacombs, but bureaucracy is. Getting official Eastwind records is a true test of patience. " He shrugged. "I'm not worried about it, though. She's good people. Anyway, can I get you something to eat?"

"In a second. I actually wanted to talk to you about something." My heart started to race again. "In private?"

His easygoing expression grew serious. "Oh, okay. Yeah. Sure. Follow me." He led me back into the kitchen, not far from the manager's office where all the trouble began. "Everything okay?" he asked, placing a strong hand on my shoulder, looking me in the eyes, and generally sending shivers all through my body.

"Yeah, everything's fine." Once he removed his hand, I was able to think again. "Actually, I just needed to ask you something. Are you aware of who the diner goes to in the event of Bruce's death?"

He flinched like I'd just flicked him on the forehead. "Um, yes." He closed his eyes. "I was wondering when that would come up."

Interesting. "How do you know?" I asked.

He shrugged guiltily. "I overheard Bruce talking about it on the phone a few weeks before he died. I wasn't trying to listen in. I was just tidying up some of the shelves during a lull and heard him shouting about it. I assume he was talking to Quinn Shaw. The guy's a little hard of hearing in his old age."

"So you didn't hear it from Seamus Shaw then?"

"Oh, sure I did. But I already knew about it by then. I honestly don't know why Quinn trusts Seamus with anything. I still had one foot outside the pub when Seamus spotted me and ran over to tell me about it."

Again with the pub. Man, could I use a beer. I made a mental note to find it as soon as I had a spare moment.

And if Tanner happened to be there at the same time, and he happened to buy me a drink, and we happened to—

Focus, Nora!

"You do realize," I began, "that your knowledge of this means you had *means*—the strength to wield a frying pan with lethal force—and *opportunity*—you were back here with Bruce when he was murdered—and now *motive*—the diner goes to you."

"You think I did it?" he asked, looking remarkably like a sad puppy.

"No, I don't," I answered truthfully. "I was here, remember? I saw your face. I've met a lot of good liars in my time, but if you were putting on a show, you'd qualify as the best I'd encountered."

Ansel's theory that anyone as likable as Tanner had to be hiding something made a certain type of sense. But I suspected that if Tanner was hiding anything, it was just how *deeply* he cared about every living being in Eastwind.

"I'm glad you don't think I'm a murderer," he said. "It's good to know I can depend on you for this."

Oh no. He depended on me? Talk about a burden to bear. Now I felt personally responsible for solving this murder so Tanner wouldn't end up in jail. I suspected the prison system in a world full of deadly paranormal creatures wasn't the kindest or most forgiving.

"So what do I do?" he said. "Just wait around for them to come arrest me?"

"No," I said, locking eyes with him. I grabbed each of his shoulders to make sure he heard what I was about to say. "You're not taking the blame for this. I know you didn't do it. So what you do now is fix me a steak and eggs to-go, then take care of this place while I figure out who murdered Bruce. Okay?"

He nodded.

Fixer of All Things wasn't my favorite role to play, but having spent so many years as a manager and owner of a restaurant, it was a role in which I was well versed. Not only had I fixed thousands of problems that my servers caused, I'd also managed to fix thousands of problems that customers conjured out of thin air. It wasn't fun, but I knew I could do it.

And Tanner's sad, desperate face was just the fuel I needed.

Also, the possible benefit of him owing me one didn't go completely ignored.

He hustled off to place the order with the cook, and I left the back-of-house and took a seat at the counter to wait.

As I looked around the place, I realized just how busy it was at this time of the morning. Was Tanner the only server? He must live his life in the weeds.

Ted was back, sitting in his same spot in the corner.

He nodded and waved. "Nora!"

Let me tell you, it never stops being creepy to hear Death call your name.

He scooted out of the booth, getting slightly tripped up on all his pitch-black robes, and approached me. I looked around quickly, and, yep, people were staring.

"How's it going, Nora?" he said, helping himself to the stool next to me.

"Oh, it's going." I smiled. Was it possible to keep this

short without upsetting him? If it was, I could do it. I was a pro at bringing small talk to a screeching halt.

But Ted wasn't great at taking hints. "Heard you stopped by Echo's yesterday."

"Yep. Sure did."

"You don't need to, you know. You're pretty enough as it is."

Oh ... no.

Death was hitting on me.

I laughed it off. "I was actually there for something else. But thanks."

"I mean it," he persisted.

"Hey, Ted," Tanner said, appearing out of nowhere like a guardian angel. "Did you need something? I can be right over. I was just busy in the back for a second."

Ted stood up, and I could hear the distinct sound of bones rattling underneath his cloak. "Nah, I'm good. Just saying hello. I'll, uh, I'll just—" He motioned back to his booth with a hitch of his thumb. "Nice to see you again, Nora."

"You too, Ted."

When I turned to look at Tanner, he inspected me with raised eyebrows and was biting back a smile.

"Stop," I said.

"Stop what?" he asked, feigning ignorance.

"You know what." I grabbed the to-go box that he'd set on the counter.

"Listen, Nora, I'm not here to judge. He *does* seem like your type, in a strange way."

"Oh shut it."

"What?" he said, holding up his hands innocently. "Plenty of women like older men. Even *much* older."

I stood. "For the record, I'm not one of those women." I set a gold coin down on the counter. "I tend to like my men a *tad* younger. That way I can teach them a thing or two."

Just before I turned my back to him, his jaw dropped. Good. My work here was done.

* * *

The unfortunate reality, as I turned onto the street where Ruby lived, was that I'd hit a dead end. Not literally. Figuratively.

I didn't know who else to talk to, was out of possible suspects, and any sane logistician would conclude, based on the facts, that Tanner Culpepper most definitely killed Bruce Saxon. If the Eastwind justice system was anything like the one back home, it would also agree with that assessment and Tanner might spend the rest of his days sharing a jail cell with some overly amorous werebear.

As I relayed the information to Grim on our walk home (omitting my interaction with Ted, obviously), he seemed even more glum than usual. *No one* wanted Tanner to take the fall for this. But the clock was ticking before an arrest would have to be made.

I dropped one of my over-medium eggs onto the porch for Grim. But before I could open the front door, I heard a man call after me. "Ms. Ashcroft."

Deputy Stu Manchester hustled over. He skipped steps as he took the stairs, and stopped abruptly only a few feet away from me. "Good morning, Ms. Ashcroft."

"Morning, Deputy."

"I have some good news," he said.

"Well then, come on in, won't you?"

He nodded and I led him inside.

Ruby was snuggled under a thick crocheted blanket in a chair in the corner of the parlor. She read a book while Bruce Saxon floated in small circles around the room to pass the time. Of course, Deputy Manchester knew nothing about Bruce's neurotic behavior, or even that he was stuck in ghost limbo.

"Deputy Manchester," Ruby said without looking up from her book. She grabbed a bookmark from the rickety table next to her chair, slipped it between the pages, placed the closed book in her lap, and carefully removed her spectacles before setting eyes on the visitor. "To what do I owe the *pleasure?*"

I didn't know Ruby well yet, but I could sense the dry sarcasm from all the way across the dimly lit room.

"Got some good news for Ms. Ashcroft here. She invited me in."

"Then come in and have a seat." She motioned to the parlor table.

"Oh, I won't be long, I don't think," he said, then he turned to me. "Just wanted to let you know that you've officially been cleared as a suspect."

"That's good," I replied. With how preoccupied I'd become finding the killer and exonerating Tanner, my own possible arrest had managed to disappear from the forefront of my mind. "Do you mind if I ask what new evidence has come to light?"

"Not so much light," said Stu, chuckling at some joke I didn't get. "More like dark. I ran into Ted this morning, out by the graveyard"—he held up a hand—"and I know what you're thinking because I was thinking it too. But no, he wasn't just milling about at the graveyard. Just a coincidence we passed there. He made that clear enough." He rolled his eyes. "And I promised him I'd let other people know if I mentioned it.

"Anyway, Ted said you couldn't be responsible for Bruce's death because he saw you sitting in a booth when he heard the sound that turned out to be the killer smashing that old cad over the back of the head."

"So much for not speaking ill of the dead," said Bruce, who hovered a foot off the ground, pretending to lean against the parlor wall. "I'm hardly a cad ..."

I ignored Bruce, though, preoccupied as I was with the new reality.

The grim reaper had lied for me. I was already in the kitchen when whoever-it-was attacked Bruce. For all Ted knew, I *was* the killer. And it didn't matter to him. Why?

The obvious reason was that he had a crush on me, but let's be honest here: I was seriously hoping for another motive. The last thing I needed on my plate was Death believing I owed him one.

"It was the last piece of the puzzle we needed," continued Deputy Manchester. "To be honest, we'd eliminated all but two suspects, you being one of them. I figured, why would Ted lie for Nora, since he doesn't know her? Anyway, now that you're eliminated, we can finally move this case forward and—" He cut himself off. "You don't seem all that relieved. If I'd just been told that I wouldn't be going to Ironhelm Penitentiary for the rest of my life, I would, I don't know, smile?"

"Sorry," I said quickly then forced a smile onto my face. "I was just ... so relieved. A little overwhelmed."

"Ah," he said, nodding and hooking his thumbs into his belt. "I forget how complex female emotions can be. Well, there you go. That was my big news. I'll just, uh, be going."

"Wait," I blurted. "You said it was down to me and one other person. And if I'm off the hook, does that mean you're making an arrest?"

"Well, not me, per se. Actually, Sheriff Bloom wanted to make the arrest herself. She knew the town wouldn't be all too happy about it. Good leader, that one. Whenever there's something extra messy, she steps in and does it herself. She should be arriving at Medium Rare as we speak, in fact."

Oh no.

"Tanner," I said, looking from Ruby to Bruce for help. I turned back to Deputy Manchester. "She's arresting Tanner?"

Stu nodded somberly. "I don't like the idea of him being a killer any more than you do, Ms. Ashcroft, but it looks awfully bad for him. Then once Seamus Shaw mentioned the will to me, well, it'll likely be another handful of months before we can get a records request through at the Parchment Catacombs, but we have probable cause for the time being. Obviously, we won't be able to use the will as official evidence until we have it secured, so Tanner will have to wait in jail for a bit. Breaks my heart to think of him going through all that, but what can you do? Murder can't go unpunished."

"Thanks, Deputy," I murmured, staring absentmindedly at a metal bauble hanging from the ceiling, catching light from the fireplace as it twisted slowly.

To the others, I might have looked like I was in shock, but I wasn't. I was hyper-focused. That happens sometimes, when problems get too big too quick. My brain blocks out everything except for the problem, which becomes a massive, cloudy blob. If I can just let it stay there for a while, undisturbed, sometimes answers emerge from the smoke.

"I'll show you out," Ruby said, crossing the room and laying a hand on Deputy Manchester's back. "Thank you so much for stopping by to deliver the news. I'm sure you have all kinds of important things to get to, though. We won't keep you a second longer."

He was already standing with both feet on the front doorstep by the time she finished speaking, and I caught a quick glimpse of Grim, out on the porch, lift his giant head, take in the scene, and then shut his eyes and lower his head again.

Ruby closed the door and set herself to making tea.

I took a seat at the table and was only faintly aware of the clinks of spoons on china as she went about her work. When I looked up again, Ruby was setting a steaming teacup in front of me, and, out of pure courtesy, I presume, she set one down in front of Bruce, too, where he hovered in a chair.

"Are we all in agreement then," she began, "that the notion of Tanner murdering Bruce is a steaming pile of unicorn swirls?"

Bruce nodded.

"Absolutely," I said. "Wait, are unicorns a thing here?"

She nodded. "There's a lovely ranch out in Erin Park. I'd bet Tanner would take you for a day trip, assuming we manage to scrounge up the evidence necessary to keep him from living the rest of his life in a dark cell with some psychopathic minotaur."

"That went from lovely to horrifying rather quickly," I said. "But you have a point."

"There's some crucial information we're missing," Ruby said. "I've been at this long enough to know when we're missing a piece." She turned to Bruce. "You said you thought it was Jane, but Nora seems fairly certain Jane wouldn't want you dead, not even in a fit of rage. Did you and Ansel ever exchange words?"

"No," Bruce said. "Ansel has a bit of a short fuse, but he and I ran together in the woods a few times before Jane and I split. We weren't best friends or anything, but we understood one another, I think. Werebears tend to be loners, and I wouldn't run with my old pack if you paid me a thousand gold coins. Those bunch of inbred, anarchists ..."

"Who?"

"My pack," he said. "Luckily, they live in the sparser parts of the Outskirts and know better than to poke their head around Medium Rare, so I never had to deal with them. Bunch of degenerates who can't get past the fact that they're not in charge in Eastwind anymore. Generations. It's been *generations* since werewolves ran this place. I got sick of telling them to get over it and finally told them I didn't want to see their mangy faces ever again."

Bad blood, by the sound of it. "Could one of them be the killer?" I asked.

"Nah," he said. "I haven't spoken to them in years. I'm dead to them. Or, um, I was dead to them before I was dead, but now I guess I'm extra dead to them." He shook his head to clear it, leaving ghastly tracers in the wake of his movement. "They live on the fringes of the Outskirts. Don't even come far enough into town to visit the diner. Not that you'd see me crying about it. They seem to think if they spend too much time in human form and around witches—no offense—it'll turn them domesticated."

Ruby turned to me. "Werewolves and witches have a long history in Eastwind. The werewolves used to run things, but the witches have since taken most of the control. And now the mayor is a witch, and not a single seat on the council is held by a werewolf. It's a touchy subject."

"Just to be clear," Bruce said, "I don't buy into that. I have no problem with witches. The witches in this town have always been nice to me, and I've done my best to return the kindness."

"What about Jane. Is she more like you or your family?" I asked.

Bruce sighed, and I could tell he still had plenty of affection for his ex-wife. "She was more like me. It was the reason we got together. Both of us were tired of the werewolf nonsense. But she came from one of the higher families. My pack was feral trash, to be blunt. She was born up in Hightower Gardens where all the old money lives. But she didn't like that life any more than I liked mine."

"Sounds like a real Romeo and Juliet story," I said, frustrated that we were no closer to helping Tanner. "Your family seems delightful and all, but I'm going to rule out speaking with them since they hate me for being a witch, and they sound like the type to enjoy a good feeding frenzy."

Bruce nodded minutely. "I don't disagree with that assessment."

Ruby chimed in. "And you said your girlfriend couldn't have done it because ...?"

"Fiona's such a sweetheart. She wouldn't hurt a jitterbug."

Ruby caught the slip, too, and we exchanged a glance. "Bruce," I said, "who's Fiona?"

"Huh?" A deep crease appeared above his nose. Then it dawned on him. "Oh. I meant Tandy."

"Nope," Ruby said curtly.

"Who's Fiona?" I demanded. "Were you *cheating* on Tandy?"

His shoulders slumped like a chastened schoolboy. "Here's the thing about Tandy. You can't just break up with a girl like that. She doesn't get it. No one breaks up with someone that beautiful. She couldn't take a hint, I'm saying. And Fiona, well, you should see her. She's a red-haired goddess." He addressed me directly with, "Not actually a goddess, just a leprechaun."

Deputy Manchester hadn't been kidding with the cad comment. "Any *other* girlfriends you might want to tell us about? Maybe one who would want you dead?"

"No," he spat. "It's not like that."

"I think it's exactly like that," I said, perturbed. "And I know you won't admit it, Bruce, but I strongly suspect you considered Jane one of those women 'you can't just break up with,' too."

"See?" said Ruby. "This is why you can't trust the deceased. When a person's reputation is all they have left, they're not keen to go spoiling it, even if it's necessary for solving their murder."

"Did Tandy know about Fiona and vice versa?" I asked.

For a moment, it looked like Bruce might clam up under the judgment. But then he shook his head. "Tandy didn't know about Fiona. Fiona knew a little bit. I told her I had a girlfriend who I'd tried to let down gently, but she wasn't getting it."

"Did Fiona know you and Tandy were still sleeping together?"

"We weren't!" he protested, but when I crossed my arms over my chest, he knew I wasn't buying it. He cringed. "No. She didn't know about that."

I took a moment to imagine being Tandy and then Fiona. I'd been those girls before—the one cheated on and the one dating the guy whose girlfriend just "couldn't take a hint." I was young and stupid then, easily fooled by whichever attractive and successful man came around and showered me with attention. I'm not proud of my mistakes and gross errors in judgment, but they were helpful in this situation.

"Tell me this, Bruce," I said, my mind starting to clear as a distinct theory took shape. "What would Fiona do if she found out you were still sleeping with Tandy?"

He pressed his lips together thoughtfully, causing tiny smoky swirls around his mouth. "I suppose she would be hurt, send me an owl saying it was over, then cry in bed for a week or so." He shrugged. "Really sensitive girl, Fiona."

"And what would Tandy do if she found out you were cheating on her?"

It was amazing how a ghost could turn even paler. His expression told me everything I needed to know, but he put the cherry on top with, "I don't even want to think about it."

"You think she would become violent?"

"I honestly don't know *what* she would do. That was half the fun with Tandy. She seems sweet and gentle, but when you get her alone,"—he whistled and it sounded like a strong breeze through a forest of decaying trees—"you never know what she's going to throw at you."

Like a frying pan?

With this new bit of information, it was all too obvious. To me, at least, and probably Ruby. But not to Bruce. "I hate to tell you this," I said, not actually hating it one bit, "but I think Tandy murdered you."

"But she didn't know," he said. "I was so careful."

Bruce was beginning to strike me as a bit dense.

"You *do* know where Tandy works, right?" I asked.

"Yeah, Echo's Salon."

I waited, but he still didn't catch where I was going. "And have you ever been in Echo's? Or any salon for that matter?"

"Of course not."

"Then allow me to fill you in. There is a *zero* percent chance that Tandy didn't hear about you and Fiona."

He sat up straight. "No! I was so careful! I made sure—"

"You're not getting it. It doesn't matter how careful you were. How long were you and Fiona together?"

He wouldn't meet my eye when he mumbled, "Six or seven months."

"Oh, for fang's sake!" Ruby said, smacking the tabletop.

I finished my tea, which was still hotter than I preferred and stood. "That settles it. Tandy knew. You said Fiona lives over in Erin Park?"

"Yeah, but you're not going to go—"

"Someone needs to warn her that she might be in danger, Bruce."

"Send an owl," he suggested.

I laughed. I couldn't help it. The idea was so ludicrous. "You want me to send an owl to someone I've never met saying, 'Don't open your door because there's a murderer loose and you might be next?' That sounds like a prank a psychopath would play on someone who'd personally wronged him."

Bruce blinked quickly. "Well, when you put it like that..."

"Before I head out, there's one thing I need to know."

"Yes?" His voice wavered like he was expecting more chastisement. Not that he didn't deserve it. But that wasn't my focus.

"What kind of creature is Tandy?" Before he responded, I added as an aside, "Oh, and is it rude to ask that of people? Because it feels like asking a stranger their sexual preference."

Ruby quickly bit back a chuckle as Bruce said, "It's a little personal, but considering you've only been here a couple days, most folks will overlook it."

"Ah, good."

"And she's a xana," he said.

Not exactly helpful, considering I had never heard that word in my life. "A what now?"

He shrugged. "She doesn't talk about it much, but it's some sort of water being. I don't honestly know much about it."

"What's her, um, power?" They all had some power, right? And subsequently, some weakness. That was how life worked, as far as I knew.

"I always assumed it was her beauty," he said. "The way men fall at her feet when she smiles at them. If that isn't a special power, I don't know what is."

Seemed kind of lame to me. Surely there had to be something else at work, otherwise she was just a beautiful woman. Texas had plenty of beautiful women, and as far as I knew, none of them were paranormal creatures.

I forced Bruce to dictate Fiona's address, which I copied down onto a small scrap of paper from Ruby's stationery box before heading out.

I had a lot of ground to cover (figuratively *and* literally), and every second I wasted was one Tanner spent staring down the business end of a wand.

Chapter Eleven

I knew the moment we set foot in the Erin Park neighborhood. For one, the people were shorter, mostly leprechauns.

How closely the leprechauns fit with my stereotypical image of a leprechaun was downright cringe-worthy. I mean, *really*. I spend my life fighting subconscious stereotyping impulses and then here come the leprechauns in their pointy green hats, green and brown clothing, and gold belts.

Any guesses about what their shoes looked like? No, it's fine, go ahead and stereotype, because you're totally correct if you say green loafers with gold buckles.

"For fang's sake," I mumbled, borrowing a phrase from Ruby.

"*Whatever you do, though,*" Grim replied, clearly following my train of thought, "*don't ever say they all look alike. They don't like that.*"

"*Don't tell me they like to brawl, too.*"

"*Er, okay, I won't tell you that.*"

"Oh gosh ... Next you're going to tell me they like to drink their weight in beer."

"I won't tell you that, either, but you might want to take a look to your left."

When I did, I realized we were passing a pub.

It was packed.

It was *maybe* one in the afternoon.

But wait, was that—

I spotted the sign. Sheehan's pub. I wondered briefly if Fiona Sheehan had any connection to it, but mostly I remembered that Tanner sometimes went there after work. Making a mental note of the location in case I wanted to drop in sometime and—oops!—bump right into Tanner, I continued following Grim down the cobblestone road, passing tiny shops and restaurants along the way.

Erin Park seemed somewhat self-contained. The emporium wasn't terribly far, but judging by the stores they kept here, they didn't need to go into the heart of Eastwind to stock up.

"*Down that street,*" Grim said, motioning with his head, "*is Rainbow Falls. The water flows down in, you guessed it, rainbows.*"

"*Water does that where I come from, too. It's called prisms.*"

A low growl rumbled from him. "*I get that you assume I don't know about prisms because I'm a dog, but I do. I'm not talking about prisms, though. I'm talking about the water actually flowing like a rainbow.*"

"*Oh. That sounds ... nice?*"

"*More like 'trying too hard.'* "

"That was actually my first thought. But I figured you might be into it."

"That doesn't sound like me," said Grim.

As we approached a row of tiny cottages, Grim trotted toward one of the porches. "This should be hers."

When the door swung open, and I laid eyes on Fiona, I was struck with a burning question: *How in god's name did Bruce hook so many beautiful women?*

He wasn't necessarily ugly, but he wasn't anything spectacular. He was bulky, but not in an athletic way so much as a dad-bod way.

He *was* confident, though. I remembered the way he'd greeted me in our one interaction before he was murdered. There was no accounting for the effect of confidence in a not-entirely-unattractive man, I supposed.

"Can I help you?" she said, looking at me puzzled.

Her puffy eyes were a good sign, insofar as she was actually sad about Bruce's death. This was how someone acts when the man they love is murdered; not what Tandy did. I couldn't believe she'd fooled me with her lame rationale.

"Hi," I said, regretting not sending an owl ahead to introduce myself. "I'm Nora. I'm, um, new in town."

She nodded slowly. Her smooth, innocent face wore a small bit of suspicion like an ill-fitting glove. "I heard about you. You were the one who found Bruce."

Before her mind could jam together puzzle pieces that didn't actually fit, I jumped in. "Yes, and that's why I'm here. I think I've figured out who did it, and I'm about to go to the police, but I think you might be in danger until that person can be arrested."

"Huh?" Her rosy cheeks drained of color, leaving her face a pale palette.

"Sorry, I don't mean to alarm you. I probably should've sent an owl ahead to let you know I was coming. I only thought of that as I was walking up to—"

"Is he yours?" she asked, pointing behind me to Grim.

"Well, he's with me, but he's not necessarily *mine*. He's, um..."

Why was I trying to hide the reality? Nobody here cared if I was a witch.

Except me.

I supposed I still felt a little like a lunatic saying *he's my familiar* aloud. But these people were used to it. And it wasn't like I would be able to hide my abilities for long. Or that there was a point to hiding them.

Sure, there was the possibility that I would have a target on my back every time someone else in Eastwind wound up murdered without seeing who the killer was. But we all have to die sometime, right?

And, apparently, I'd already died once. That meant I had more experience with it than just about anyone else in this town. Except Grim and Ruby. And, of course, Ted.

"He's my familiar," I said, trying to sound unashamed, if not proud.

"Oh," she said, nodding. "That makes sense. Ruby True has a dog familiar, too. Does that mean you're one of those Fifth Wind witches, too?"

"Yeah, it does."

"Neat." She smiled acceptingly, then suddenly her

expression changed and she looked like *she'd* just seen a ghost. "Wait, did you talk to Bruce?"

Oh boy. "Yes."

"A-a-and did he talk about me?"

Ready, set, bald-faced lie! "Talk about you? He won't shut up about you! I would've come sooner, but I was swamped."

I don't know why I thought that would cheer up Fiona. It was like my brain temporarily forgot how sensitive people behaved.

The waterworks were in full force with that one when I glanced behind me at Grim.

"Smooth move, there," he hollered telepathically. *"I have literally spent my entire life in the Deadwoods, cut off from society, and I could've told you not to say that."*

"What was I supposed to say? 'He didn't mention you until he accidentally called his other girlfriend by your name'? Would that have been better?"

"It couldn't have been worse."

As her crying subsided, I remembered that every second I spent here was a second Tanner spent in who knew where. In lockup? In an interrogation room with a spotlight pointed in his eyes? Did they have habeas corpus here?

With a final reminder to keep her door locked and, until she heard from me, not answer it for anyone, not even someone she thought she knew well, I followed Grim toward the sheriff's department.

Chapter Twelve

"*Just come in with me,*" I urged Grim. "*They let werewolves in here, so why not a dog?*"

On the front steps of the modest sheriff's office, Grim planted his feet. "*No way. Of all the buildings to go into, I'm not picking the police station.*"

"*They're not going to arrest a dog, Grim.*"

"*You don't know that. I might seem like witch's best friend to you now, but out in the Deadwoods ... I've done some things, Nora. Things I'm not proud of. Things I can never take back.*"

"*Oh, for fang's sake.*" I threw my arms into the air. "*I'm not buying the bad-dog act, okay?*"

"*Suit yourself. Why exactly do you want me to go in there?*"

Was he really going to make me say it? I tried to wait him out, but, yep, he was going to make me say it. "*Because I trust your judgment. You were right about Ansel, and you obviously like Tanner, based on the way you let him really get in there behind your ears—*"

"I thought we weren't going to talk about that ever again."

"Come on, Grim. I need you."

He yapped a laugh. *"You need me?"*

"Psh, no. I mean, not need *you* need you, *but you've proven yourself to be not entirely unhelpful."*

"When you put it in such flattering terms,"—he lowered himself onto the top step—*"good luck in there, kid. I know you'll do great."*

"Oh, come on." I paused, strategizing. *"If you come with me, I'll buy you another lasagna at Franco's Pizza afterward."*

With great effort, he lifted himself off the ground. *"I guess that's acceptable,"* he said nonchalantly.

But I could see the drool pooling at the edge of his floppy jowls.

"Well, if it isn't Ms. Ashcroft," said Deputy Manchester when I approached the reception desk. I must've interrupted him chatting with the receptionist, and the two of them watched unabashedly as Grim and I approached. "It's been all of two hours since we parted ways."

The receptionist was a short, pudgy man. Back in Texas, I would have felt guilty for thinking, *Wow, he looked like a goblin,* but in Eastwind, I thought I might be spot on. What creature I was currently dealing with didn't matter, though, so I didn't bother asking.

"I go and tell you that you're off the hook and you come into the sheriff's office anyway?" He turned to the receptionist. "Some women just can't take a hint, huh?" They shared a laugh at my expense.

Fine. Laugh away. I wasn't here to make friends.

I mean, yeah, it would've been nice if they weren't sitting around laughing at me, but whatever. "I need to speak with Sheriff Bloom," I said.

"Great," said Stu. "Jingo can help you with that." He nodded at the short man. "My guess is she'll have some availability next month."

"It can't wait. They have the wrong person. Tanner didn't kill Bruce."

"And you know this how?" Stu asked, sounding mostly disinterested. "Were you together when the murder took place?" He wagged a finger at me. "That's it, isn't it? I could tell *something* was up between you two the moment I walked in." He filled in Jingo. "You could cut the sexual tension with a knife." He mimed just such a thing for effect. "Were you two getting up to a little hocus-pocus in the supply closet?" He grinned lecherously. "You were, weren't you? I *knew* it!"

"What," I began, "in God's name are you talking about?"

His mirth came to a screeching halt. "Huh?"

"We weren't ... there was no hocus-pocus going on."

But also, was there that much sexual tension?

No, of course not. When Deputy Manchester arrived on scene, we were both most definitely not thinking about that. We'd just seen a dead body, for fang's sake!

Deputy Manchester resumed a professional composure. "Then how, may I ask, can you claim he didn't do it?"

"I need to talk to Sheriff Bloom."

"I understand that," he said, enunciating each syllable like it might help my slow brain understand. "But like I already told you, she's busy until at least Ostara."

"I don't know what Ostara is, and I don't care."

"*It's our spring festival,*" Grim said. "*It happens every March, but the specific day varies—*"

"*I didn't bring you to be my Wikipedia, Grim.*"

"Fine. Put me on the calendar," I said, addressing Jingo.

Leaning over the desk, I pointed to an open slot on his parchment. "What's that?" I asked.

"What?" he said.

"That. What does that mean? Is that something to do with Deputy Manchester's schedule?"

At hearing his name, the deputy also leaned over the desk to see what I was pointing at.

If you guessed "nothing," you're correct. But they both fell for it.

As the two men squinted to figure out what I was talking about, I scanned the area behind them until I spotted what I was looking for.

"*Grim. I need you to cause a distraction.*"

"*Like what?*"

"*I don't know. Anything. Just cause a little bit of chaos. Can you do that?*"

He trotted to the opposite side of the desk from Manchester and lifted his leg. "*You kidding? I was born for this.*"

Grim's forceful pee stream splashed loudly on the wooden desk.

"Wha— Ohhh come on!" shouted Jingo in a gravelly voice.

When Deputy Manchester leaned to the side to look, I saw my window. "*Pace yourself. I need a couple minutes.*"

"*No need. I was born to leave my mark on the world. I've got a bottomless tank.*"

I hustled to the door with the wood engraving that read *Sheriff Gabrielle Bloom* and pushed it open without knocking.

As soon as I oriented myself, I realized I'd committed a gross oversight.

I had no idea what kind of creature the sheriff was. What if she hated witches? What if she was a sphinx and started asking me riddles and if I couldn't answer one she ate me? I was terrible at riddles.

The U-shaped desk was piled so high with papers that I almost didn't see the top of her head as she stooped over in her chair.

When she looked up at me, I felt a mixture of calm and guilt wash over me.

And for some reason, a memory of stealing a cookie from my aunt and blaming it on the kids next door surfaced in my mind. Weird.

"May I help you?" she asked.

Her face was lean, blonde hair in a pixie cut.

Did that mean she was a pixie?

No, probably not.

The dang leprechauns had sent me into a downward spiral of stereotyping.

I shut the door behind me so Stu wouldn't see where I was once the initial shock of Grim's powerful bladder wore off.

I stepped forward cautiously. "I need to talk to you about Bruce Saxon's murder."

She narrowed her eyes at me for a moment, then relaxed. "You must be Nora Ashcroft."

"Yes, ma'am."

"And you just burst into my office because?"

"Tanner is innocent."

She sighed heavily. "Come, have a seat."

I looked at the papers stacked on every surface. "Where?"

She stood, and when she did, I glimpsed the wings.

If I didn't know any better, I'd guess Sheriff Bloom was an angel. And before I could think better of it, I blurted, "Are you an angel?"

As she moved a stack of papers from the chair in front of her desk to the ground, she chuckled. "What gave it away? Was it the giant, white wings?"

Okay, yeah. That one was on me.

"Sorry," she said quickly. "You're new. I've met plenty of new people in my time, so I know there's an adjustment period." She motioned to the empty chair. "There, now you can have a seat."

After clearing off a small gap in the wall of paperwork so that I could see her over her desk, she placed clasped hands in her lap and said, "I know Tanner is innocent."

"You do?"

"Yes."

"How?"

"It's part of being an angel. I can tell who's innocent and whose soul is tainted by lies. Makes me quite good at interrogations. Unfortunately, it's never that simple. When I sense dishonesty, *I* may know on a core level that it's because the person committed the crime of which they're being accused, but my ability to sense those things doesn't hold up in a court of law."

"So you talked to Tanner and think he's innocent?"

Her posture softened and her wings slumped. "There are few people in this town *more* innocent than Tanner Culpepper. I know that. But the High Council has been on me about closing this case, and all the evidence points to him. I had to make an arrest."

"But you know it's not him! That means the person who did it is still out there. They could kill again."

She shook her head, disheartened. "I know. But look around you, Nora. Look at this paperwork I have to sort through. It's unrealistic. I can never be as thorough as I'd like to. I have to close cases wherever I can."

"What if I told you I knew who actually killed Bruce?"

She tilted her head to the side. "I'd ask you what proof you have?"

"Um, yes, I don't have that yet. But I think, with your help, I can get it."

She frowned. "In a way that wouldn't necessitate entrapment? The Council isn't huge on that."

"That makes sense. I don't know how I'll get the evidence, but I'm determined to do it. Correct me if I'm wrong, but neither of us wants to see Tanner in prison for a crime he didn't do."

Her gaze roamed the piles of parchment, and she sighed. "It's not like the paperwork is going to run off if I take a couple hours off to exonerate an innocent man." Her wings stretched out behind her, knocking over a precariously balanced stack and causing a domino effect as papers cascaded to the floor. She didn't seem to care. "For heaven's sake! Let's do this. Who do you suspect?"

I tried not to get overexcited, but it seemed like this might actually happen.

I opened my mouth to explain when I heard Stu's irate voice outside the door. "Don't tell me Ms. Ashcroft went in *there!*"

The door burst open, and Deputy Manchester stood on the threshold, red-faced. "Ms. Ashcroft! I—"

I gasped as the door slammed shut in his face.

Sheriff Bloom lowered her arm, which was extended toward the door, and returned her attention to me. "You were saying?"

O-kay ... Angels could move things with a flick of their wrist. Noted.

"Um, I don't know what I was ... Oh right! The murderer. It was Tandy."

"Tandy Erixon? Who works down at Echo's Salon?"

"Yes. She was dating Bruce."

"I know. Pretty sure *everyone* in Eastwind knows, considering the display those two put on." She pressed her lips together and shook her head disapprovingly. "Go on."

"Bruce was also dating Fiona Sheehan."

Bloom leaned back in her chair. "Ah."

We exchanged a knowing glance, and the matter was settled. No further explanation needed. And I couldn't help but feel relieved that this town had a female sheriff.

Two thin lines appeared at the bridge of her nose, and she chewed her bottom lip before asking, "What kind of creature is Tandy? I can't recall."

"A xana."

A small twitch of her head. "A what?"

"A xana. Wait, are you telling me you don't know what that is?"

"Not afraid to admit what I don't know. Plus," she added airily, "God Herself couldn't keep up with all the different types of beings in Eastwind. And all of them think their breed is superior." She rolled her eyes. "Anyway, no, I'm not sure what a xana is, but if we're going to act on this suspicion of yours, which seems as solid a hunch as any, we need to know what we're up against."

Searching the office for anything that might resemble a computer, I came up empty-handed. "And where do we find that?"

"The library," she said, grabbing a coat on her way to the office door.

She slipped it on and a moment later her wings emerged from two tailored slits down the back.

I had to hustle to keep up with her pace as she crossed the station, breezing by a stunned Deputy Manchester and passed the front desk.

"Grim," I said, spotting him still in hiked position. "Let's go."

"I can't just cut it off midstream," he protested.

I stopped in my tracks. *"You're not done yet?"*

"I told you! This was the role I was born to play."

I grabbed him by the scruff of his neck, careful to avoid any splashes from his continuing trickle, and dragged him behind me and out of the sheriff's office.

"If they didn't allow dogs before," I told him as we descended the stairs out front, *"they definitely won't allow them now."*

Chapter Thirteen

The Eastwind Library was a hulking structure only a few blocks away from the sheriff's office. Imposing arches and stone gargoyles loomed over approaching visitors, making me wonder, of course, if there were actual gargoyles in Eastwind.

Growing up, I'd always loved bookstores, but for some reason, libraries had given me the creeps. As soon as Sheriff Bloom and I set foot on the marble floors of the Eastwind library, Grim a few steps behind, I formulated a theory as to why I'd never felt comfortable in libraries.

The place was teeming with ghosts. Ruby had a theory that I'd always been able to sense ghosts, but my mind and body weren't fully open to them until I crossed into Eastwind. If that were the case and Texas libraries were anything like this, it made sense why I'd avoided them whenever possible.

The spirits floated this way and that from one aisle to the next. Ghosts filled the empty chairs on either side of long wooden tables that were lit by floating lamps every yard or so down the center and stretched the length of the colossal first floor. Like Bruce, the ghosts hovered slightly above the chairs, sitting out of habit, I assumed, rather than any actual need.

It took a minute before I noticed something especially strange going on. Whereas Bruce hadn't been able to touch the teacup Ruby set out for him, these ghosts were not only able to turn the pages of the books that sat open before them, they were also able to take the books off the shelves and move them. I tried to imagine what it would look like to someone who couldn't see spirits. The books would appear to float through thin air. That would be weird.

Although, not as weird as seeing a bunch of ghosts.

"Is it always this packed?" I asked Grim.

"Your guess is as good as mine. I've never bothered coming in here. I can't read. Because I'm a dog."

"Excuses, excuses," I said, already tuning him out again.

Sheriff Bloom dodged the floating books but didn't seem too worried about the accompanying ghosts carrying them from place to place. As she cut across the chamber, she passed through one spirit after another without flinching.

"You can't see them, I assume?" I asked.

"The books, yes. The restless spirits, no. But I can feel them, sometimes pure, sometimes … not so pure."

And I thought *I* could be a little on the judgmental side.

The sheriff knew her way around the place. She must come here a lot. It made sense. If I had that much paperwork to fill out and worked in the same building as someone like Stu Manchester, I'd probably come somewhere deserted (except for the ghosts, obviously) to knock out my work without the possibility of unnecessary distraction.

We paused between two long rows of shelves, and Bloom leaned forward toward a waist-high shelf. "Let's see ... Were-elk, werewolf, will-o'-the-wisp"—she dragged her finger along the spines of books as she read them off—"wolpertinger, wraith, wyrm—ah! Here we go. Xana."

She pulled a thick leather book from the dusty shelf with *ancestry* scrawled in it, and turned to the table of contents before flipping through. Her eyes scanned from top to bottom so rapidly that I assumed she was just scanning. But then she flipped the page, did the same over and over again, then shut the book. "Well, this is interesting."

"Did you actually read all that?"

"Yes. When you have as many documents to look over as I do and thousands of years to hone your skills, you learn how to speed read."

Thousands of years? I'd have to ask about that later.

"So what'd you find?"

"You met Tandy in person, right?"

"Yes."

"And when you spoke with her, did you *hear* anything out of the ordinary?"

"Um, no. Not that I..." Then it came back to me. "Actually, I remember music. The harp. Is that what—"

"And how did it sound to you?"

"I don't know. Like a harp? You probably know more about the harp than I do."

"Why do you say that?" She appeared genuinely stumped.

"Because you're an— Never mind. Why are we talking about the music?"

"Did you enjoy it or did it irritate you in any way?"

"I enjoyed it. It was actually one of the most beautiful pieces I've ever heard."

Sheriff Bloom beamed. "Yes, that's what I thought you'd say, but I had to be sure. Hmm ..." She opened the book again, staring down at it as she worried her bottom lip.

"Are you going to explain?"

She cleared her head with a shake and shut the book again. "Oh right. Xana, as the book explains, can produce a song. They can direct it at a specific target. If the target is pure of heart, the music sounds beautiful. In your case, you heard a harp and you found it enjoyable. That bodes well for you."

"But?"

"*But* if the person is impure or lying or hiding something, the song can slowly drive them insane, causing paranoia and even hallucinations."

Well, then. I was glad I passed the test. I'd once eaten an old mushroom pizza that gave me hallucinations. I didn't want to relive that experience, especially in a town that already felt a little like one extended drug trip.

Besides, it was hard enough to be the new girl in town. The last thing I needed was to be stumbling around town all twitchy and talking to people who weren't there.

A tiny memory knocked on the inside of my skull. "Hold up," I said, retrieving it. "Tanner said something about— Yes! That's it! Tanner said Bruce was acting strange in the week leading up to the murder. Talking to people who weren't there and being paranoid. Do you think ...?"

Bloom chuckled dryly. "Oh yeah. I definitely think."

"But how do we know?"

Bloom replaced the book on the shelf. "That's the catch. We can arrest her, but without evidence, the charges won't stick. If she confesses, then we might have something, but she doesn't strike me as the type to confess. If we did somehow manage to make the charges stick and she went to trial, that wouldn't turn out the way we want it, either; put someone who looks like her in front of a jury, and you're going to get a verdict of innocent every single time."

Sounded like the justice system in Eastwind wasn't a far cry from the one back home.

"So we trick her?" I asked.

"Nooo ..." she said firmly. "That could easily be misconstrued by a jury. At least if *I* do it. However, if you were to find evidence or have her confess when an officer of the law just happened to be around to witness it ..." She let the words hang, which was fine. She didn't need to say more.

"So the question becomes, how do you convince a psycho like that to show her true colors?" I said.

"That's the million-gold-piece question, right there."

Having gotten the answers we came for (other than a specific how-to of tricking Tandy, which I didn't suspect even a library this massive would contain), we passed through one freezing-cold ghost after another and made for the front steps of the library.

"I have to get back to the paperwork," she said, "but

I'll postpone moving forward with Tanner as long as I can. And I'll make sure he's treated well while in our custody. You just send an owl to let me know where you need Deputy Manchester to be and when, and I'll send him along."

"You trust him?"

"Manchester?" she said, caught off guard. "Of course I do." Then her temporary shock diminished, and she amended with, "Sure, he can be a little full of himself and unintentionally patronizing, but trust me when I say he has a good heart. Sensing that is sort of *my thing*."

"Okay. If you trust him, I trust him."

"He's a good cop. Reliable, honest. He may be a pain in the hide sometimes, but he comes through in the clutch. And that's what matters. We're a small department. Not including Jingo, who isn't worth his weight in sage when it comes to customer service, it's just Manchester and me in charge of all law and order in this town. I'd trust him with my life. That is, if I were mortal." She shrugged before leaning over to Grim. "Don't let her get into trouble. And also, be sure to hydrate thoroughly after that stunt you pulled on Jingo's desk."

She patted him on the head then headed back to the station.

"Let's get out of here," I said. "You ready for that lasagna?"

"*Am I!*" As he padded down the steps and I recapped the information I'd just learned about xana, a question formed in my mind. "*Hey Grim, out of curiosity, did you hear Tandy's song at all when we were at Echo's Salon?*"

"*No, but if I did, I'm sure it would've sounded worse than a banshee's nails on a pewter cauldron.*"

I rolled my eyes. "Yeah, yeah. You have such a dark past. Give me one example of something terrible you've done."

"Nuh-uh. Not happening. What happens in the Deadwoods never sees the light of day."

Oh boy. "I really lucked out when I got you as my familiar," I said sarcastically.

"I was just thinking the same about you. Keep in mind, though, that not all luck is good luck."

"Oh, I am, Grim. I am."

Chapter Fourteen

Franco's Pizza was much busier in the late afternoon, and the familiar clank of metal and glass, and the excited and friendly chatter felt like a small slice of home. I didn't so much miss the pressure of running Chez Coeur, but I did miss this.

When you live most of your life alone, or at least feeling alone and going unnoticed and unappreciated, any proof that you exist and are a part of something larger, that this world is real and alive and you're a piece of it, is like wrapping yourself in a thick comforter on a chilly November night.

Grim wanted to stay outside, and I didn't fight him on it. The host stand was now occupied by a sweet willowy girl, perhaps in her late teens, with dark mocha skin and dazzling green eyes. "Welcome," she said. "Table for one?"

"Just want to place an order to-go, actually. And is Jane in?"

"Yes."

"May I speak with her?"

The hostess's gentle childlike demeanor transitioned rapidly into the teenage skepticism I'd always appreciated. "Uh, are you sure you want to?"

I laughed. "Yes, I'm sure."

She gave a suit-yourself shrug. "What's your name, so I can let her know?"

"Nora Ashcroft."

The recognition was immediate.

I always thought having my reputation precede me would be kind of cool. But as it turns out, it was a little creepy and unsettling.

"Oh, *you're* Nora?"

"Yep."

"I heard about you."

Obviously. "From who?"

"My uncle. He said you came by where he worked and started asking questions about Bruce Saxon."

"Ah. Ansel? He's your uncle?"

She nodded.

"And what's your name?"

"Greta."

"Nice to meet you, Greta. Do I order from you, or ...?"

"At the bar," she said, visibly more relaxed now that we'd exchanged names.

I may not know how to use a wand or cast spells, but the affability that simply asking for a person's name can conjure might as well be a magic trick.

"I'll tell Jane to find you there."

"Great. Thanks, Greta."

Much to my superficial delight, the sexy bartender

was working away, waving his wand around like some Hogwarts alum as a bottle of red wine glided over three glasses, pouring into each without a drop spilled.

I admit, in that moment, I had serious wand envy.

I took the last empty chair at the bar and smiled at him when he glanced my way.

He looked right past me.

I chalked it up to the amount of focus such magical multitasking required until his eyes locked onto something over my shoulder and shouted, "Pablo! Good to see you!" while waving with his non-wand hand.

When he glanced my way again a few moments later, I cleared my throat and raised a finger casually signal that I needed service.

Again, no dice.

"Excuse me," I finally called, agitated. I hadn't planned on grabbing a drink this early in the day, but if he kept ignoring me, I would definitely want a glass of wine. Or better yet, a couple fingers of whiskey.

Oh no. Did they have whiskey in Eastwind?

They had leprechauns, right? Undeniably stereotypical leprechauns, nonetheless. They *had* to have whiskey, or something just like it, right?

"What do you need, Nora?" the deep, smooth voice yanked me out of my alcoholic concerns, and I focused on Sexy Bartender, who'd finally decided to acknowledge my existence.

"You know my name?"

"Of course. You're the one who got Tanner arrested."

"I did *not*," I insisted.

"Sure, whatever." He continued flicking his wand

around, and empty glasses on the bar floated into a bucket of soapy water.

"I want to place an order to-go."

"Aww, so sad you're not staying," he said flatly.

"I don't know that I like you."

"Does that mean I can expect Sheriff Bloom to show up here and arrest me sometime soon, too?"

My response got tangled up in my throat, which was probably for the best since it was composed entirely of four-letter words.

"Nora."

(No, my name wasn't one of them.)

Jane sauntered up, smiling. "Good to see you back here so soon."

I should have said hello and mentioned that the lasagna was too good to stay away, but instead I said, "Did you know your bartender is kind of a jerk?"

Her eyes jumped to him then back to me. "Yes."

"Oh. Well, um, he's refusing to serve me."

"Am not," he said. "You never placed an order."

"Because you never asked me what I wanted!"

"Donovan," she said smoothly, "we like Nora, okay?"

He shrugged in a petulant way that would've looked more natural on Greta than a grown man. "I don't care about her either way, to be honest. She's just Tanner's little crush who got him arrested, far as I'm concerned."

The accusation bounced right off me this time, because, um, hold the phones—I was "Tanner's little crush"? Did Donovan know that for sure, or was he just assuming?

"She's also the person," Jane countered, "who's working her butt off to solve my ex-husband's murder and thereby get Tanner out of custody, so I'd appreciate if you checked that annoyingly sexy, tortured attitude at the host stand, you hear?"

Donovan appeared cowed, and I'm not ashamed to admit I enjoyed seeing it.

He didn't look at Jane as he said, "Yeah, I hear."

"Now get her a drink on the house." She nodded at me. "What's your potion?"

I scanned the setup of bottles, but none of them were labeled. "Do you have whiskey?"

Jane grinned. "Boy, do we."

"I could do with a nice winter whiskey cocktail."

Jane nodded approvingly. "Donovan, get her a spiced yeti, and use the Sheehan twelve-year whiskey." She nodded at me. "And to eat?"

"A lasagna to-go, please." My stomach growled. Oh right. I guess I should get myself something. "Make it two."

"Two?" She sounded impressed, but I knew she misunderstood.

"Not both for me. One for me, and one for Grim."

"Your familiar?"

"Yeah, the big black dog out there staring pitifully through the window, hoping it'll earn him some scraps."

"Donovan," she hollered. "Put in an order for two lasagnas to-go."

He bit back whatever sulky response was struggling to free itself from his thick, perfect lips, and scrawled the order in the air with his wand, wispy cursive tracers following the movements.

"Taking good care of that dog, huh?" Jane asked.

"Well, he did me a solid at the sheriff's office earlier." More like a liquid.

"I like dog people," she said. "I'm one myself."

The corners of her mouth twitched, and when I caught her double meaning, I wasn't able to hold back the laughter, and as I erupted, so did she.

The fairy servers flit around from table to table, and as I watched, my mind returned to why I had actually come here, aside from my deal with Grim. "I have a favor to ask, Jane."

"Yes?" Her demeanor tightened. She probably wasn't used to people asking her for favors. She didn't exactly radiate warmth.

"You said you had a friend who works at Echo's Salon, right?"

"Yeah, Hyacinth Bouquet."

I leaned forward to avoid being overheard. "Do you think you could get her to spread a bit of hand-crafted gossip around the salon?"

"I don't think I could stop her from doing it, honestly."

"Perfect."

Donovan slammed my cocktail down on the bar in front of me then disappeared again.

When Jane opened her mouth to scold him, I held up a hand. "Let him sulk. I don't care." The warm glass in my hand relaxed me, and that first sip ... Oh holy smokes.

I mean, literally. The smokiness was divine. I knew enough about cocktails to credit that to the whiskey at the heart of the drink. There had to be magic involved in the distillation process. And lots of it.

I took another sip. Then help up the glass to inspect

it. My guess was whiskey, warmed cream, cinnamon, cloves and—I took another sip—was that a splash of maple syrup?

It could have been a splash of Grim's pee, and I still would've drunk it.

Well, okay, maybe that's too far.

But you get the picture.

"Good?" asked Jane.

"If whiskey tasted this good where I came from, it would immediately be made illegal."

"I hope I never end up where you came from, then." She allowed me another moment of silence with my drink before jumping in. "So what do you need me to feed to Hyacinth?"

"Oh right. That." It all seemed so unimportant now that the spiced yeti was in my life. But, like a champ, I pushed through. "I need it to get around that I know who the murderer is and that I'm going to speak with Sheriff Bloom about it first thing in the morning. Also, it's crucial that people think I already have the evidence."

Jane's eyes opened wide. "Do you? Know who the murder is, I mean."

I nodded subtly. "Yes." I looked around the room. Who knew what sort of creatures around here had super hearing. I couldn't risk it. "But I shouldn't say just yet. Can you make sure Hyacinth hears about this before the salon closes for the evening? It's vitally important that it has enough time to make it around."

"Oh, don't worry about that," she said, waving me off. "Rumors don't need time to spread at Echo's. It's in one ear out the mouth. *Stemming* the flow is a trick all the witches in Eastwind couldn't pull off even if they put their wands together. By the way, why don't you have a wand? You're a witch, right?"

"I'm actually not sure where I stand on the whole wand thing. Or the witch thing."

"You should probably figure that out," she suggested.

"Your lips to God's ears." I finished my cocktail just as a raven-haired fairy flew out of the kitchen carrying a to-go bag with the food. I reached into my pocket and pulled out a handful of the gold coins. "How much do I owe you?"

Jane looked down and gasped. "Ooo, Nora, you better tuck that right back into your pocket."

"Oh come on, you have to let me pay. You're already doing me a favor."

She closed my fingers around the gold and pushed my hand back toward my pants. "I'll let you pay, but that's *way* too much money. You can't just pull out a fistful of gold in public. People have wound up dead for less."

"Oh." Since no one in this town had let me pay for a thing so far—well, except Tanner, but I'd simply set the gold piece on the counter and walked out—I hadn't realized that Ruby had slipped me a small fortune.

"Just one of those will work," Jane said, "and he'll bring you change. Lots of change."

"No change. Keep it."

She smiled maternally, though she was likely only a decade my senior. "I'll apply it as credit. You can eat here every day for the next year on that."

"Oh, dang. I— Wow."

Apparently, Ruby was loaded. Maybe medium-turned-private-investigator was a lucrative business.

When I moved toward the door, Jane grabbed my hand. "I get the feeling whatever you're planning is dangerous. So now *you* do *me* a favor."

"Okay?"

"Don't get yourself killed. I happen to like you."

Chapter Fifteen

It took some convincing, but Ruby allowed Grim to enter the house without first having a bath ... this one time. It was special circumstances, after all. I was wading into dangerous waters, and I needed unassuming backup in case things went south.

Ruby had taken Clifford out for an evening stroll at my request. That, however, didn't take much convincing. She didn't want to be anywhere near when the confrontation inevitably went down. Said her nerves had been through enough in her many years.

So I was left alone in the parlor, waiting for a knock at the door.

Well, not entirely alone. Grim was snoozing by a fireplace, being more dog than tortured soul for once, and Bruce Saxon lounged in Ruby's chair in the corner, staring longingly at a book he couldn't open to read. Apparently, ghosts could only move the books when they were in the library. I chalked that up to more magic I didn't understand.

And then there was Deputy Stu lying in wait ...

When the last light faded through the crack in the curtains, a knock on the door echoed through the cozy first floor. I inhaled deeply, shoring up courage, and went to answer it. But I paused before opening the door. This was the first really dangerous part. She could surprise me, try to overpower me immediately, whop me over the head with something heavy like she did Bruce.

"Grim," I hissed.

He snorted awake from his slumber. *"What?"*

"Would you mind staying conscious for just a little longer?"

"Fine. But next time you need me to be alert, don't set an entire lasagna in front of me a couple hours before."

"You knew this was coming. You could've paced yourself." But even as I said it, I knew it wasn't true. Grim might be my familiar, but he was still a dog, and I'd never known one to have any self-control when people food was on offer.

I swallowed hard and opened the door, my muscles tensing for the worst.

Instead, Tandy beamed at me like we were old friends. "Nora! So good to see you again!"

Hyacinth had done her job. "Hey, Tandy. What brings you here at this hour?"

"Oh, you know, just wanted to stop by. I was the new girl in town once, and I know how hard it can be when you don't know anyone. Thought I'd drop by and get to know you better."

Man oh man, I bet people fell for her nice act all the time. Even I found it difficult to look at someone like her and think "murderer," and I believed with some certainty that she'd done it.

"Great," I said. "Come on in."

I stepped to the side and she glided into Ruby's house.

Bruce floated a few feet closer to her so that the flames of the fireplace flickered through him, making it difficult to see his lower half. "I'm sorry," he said, "but I still don't buy it. There's no way Tandy would do it."

I flashed him a sharp look, warning him not to get any closer in case she felt the cold chill of his presence, put the pieces together, and blew our plan to smithereens.

"Tea?" I said as she settled at the parlor table.

"Yes, please."

I set to making it just like I'd seen Ruby do.

I paused, staring down at the jars of dried leaves, twigs, and blossoms. Hmm ... which were the ones for tea and which were for what few spells Ruby could perform? It seemed important not to mix up the two categories.

I went with the largest pot that I was sure I'd seen her scoop out of before. Then I added a sprinkle from a small wooden box, which I was sure held dried lavender. I could tell dried lavender just by touch alone, I'd used it in so many recipes at Chez Coeur.

As I stoked the stove with a few hickory chips and set the pot of water on top, Tandy struck up conversation.

"What have you been up to since you arrived in Eastwind?"

"Oh, nothing much," I said. "Just seeing the town, mostly. Everything here is so different than where I come from."

"And where is that, exactly?"

"Texas. Austin, to be precise."

"Never heard of it," she said quickly.

"No one here has. Except Ruby. You said you weren't from Eastwind?" The tea kettle began to whine, and I pulled it off and poured it into two cups, thankful that water boiled almost instantly here—why, though, I wasn't sure. It was probably best if I stopped wondering how magic worked.

"Right. I'm originally from Avalon."

"Is that ... near here?"

She laughed airily. "Not particularly. You can get there through an archway outside of town, but I think physically, the two places aren't nearby. Frankly, I'm not even sure they're in the same realm."

I had questions. So many questions. But they were all off topic, and the last thing I needed was this whole thing to lead nowhere and for Deputy Manchester to have spent the evening hiding in Ruby's bathroom for nothing.

So we're clear, I did *not* put all my eggs in the Grim basket when it came to my personal safety. Besides, any confession was pointless if neither Manchester nor Bloom was around to hear it. That's why I'd sent an owl to Bloom, as she suggested, and she'd passed the order down to her deputy.

Manchester had been waiting patiently for an hour for Tandy to show up, and I could only imagine the look on his face as he slowly realized I might be right about Tanner's innocence.

"Is it common for people from Avalon to come to Eastwind?" I asked, setting the tea in front of her and taking the seat next to hers at the round table.

"No," she said, furtively. "Eastwinders may want to

visit Avalon, but Avalonians don't usually want to come here."

"So, why did you?"

"I happen to like the small-town feel. I don't find the poverty off-putting like the rest of Avalon does."

Poverty? That wasn't how I'd describe Eastwind at all. Avalon must be a seriously pretentious place. Zoe Clementine had said as much.

"So you came because ...?"

"I met Echo Chambers at a soiree back home, and he convinced me to come work for him in Eastwind." She swiped at the memory with the back of her hand, as if it held no interest for her anymore. "What did you do before you came here?"

"Ran a restaurant." I sipped my tea slowly, gauging her reaction.

She feigned surprise. "Oh really? That's not what I would have guessed." Flipping her hair behind her shoulder, she leaned forward and tasted her tea.

"What would you have guessed?"

She shrugged a single shoulder bashfully. "Oh, I don't know. There was just gossip around the salon about what you've been up to, and with the long coat and complete disregard for makeup, well, I thought you might have been a detective."

Bingo. Here we were. All the conversation leading up to this point had been idle small talk, foreplay leading into the good nitty-gritty.

My heart raced, but I kept my hands steady, gripping my tea cup. "A detective?"

"Oh, yes. And if the rumors are true, you're fairly

good at it. Word around Echo's is that you've solved Bruce's murder."

"Yes," I said plainly, keeping my eyes locked onto hers. "I have."

"So, who was it?" she said, just a little too cheerily. "No wait, let me guess. Ansel?"

I shook my head. "No, not him."

"Hmm ..." She tapped a perfectly manicured finger to her soft pale-pink lips. "Okay, then it had to be Jane."

"Nope."

The silence was thick between us.

And then faint harp music filled the air.

"I stand by what I said," Bruce interjected. "She's not my murderer. The murderer wouldn't be guessing who the murderer is."

Not to be too harsh, but this was exactly why Bruce was dead. He was too big of a sucker for a pretty face. He didn't want to believe she could do such a thing, so he hadn't prepared for the event like I had.

"Do you hear it, Grim?" I asked.

"Hear what, the harp?"

"Aha! I knew it."

"What? No! You, um, didn't let me finish ... I was going to say 'harpy chorus,' because that's what I'm hearing right now. Awful. It's like my ears are bleeding."

The tinkle of Tandy's teacup landing on its saucer pulled my attention back to the crucial task at hand. "Do you have evidence?" she asked.

"Yes," I replied. "Looks pretty damning." I flashed her a fake grin, making it obvious that there was no congeniality behind it. I wanted her to know that I knew. I needed her to feel trapped.

"Are you going to tell me what the evidence is?" she asked.

"No, I think I'm going to save it for Sheriff Bloom in the morning."

She inhaled deeply, staring down at her cup. "Have you ever been cheated on, Nora?"

"Of course. Who hasn't?"

"Then you know," she said without looking up. "Oh look, I'm out of tea."

"I'll get you some more."

"No." She rose quickly. "I can get it."

I tried to remain calm without taking my eyes off of her.

"Guilt eats at people," she said from just a few yards away in the adjoined kitchen. "In the end, our guilt catches up with us."

"Do you have something to feel guilty about, Tandy?"

She returned with a full cup and the kettle. "Top up?"

"Sure. Thanks."

She poured for me and set the kettle onto a small pot holder on the table beside her.

"I wasn't talking about my own guilt," she said. "I was talking about Bruce's."

"Bruce's guilt? For what? What'd he do?"

She grinned at me, and a sliver of pearly teeth cut through the gentle beauty of her face like a knife. "If you've solved the murder like you say you have, you already know.

"I, on the other hand, only suspected. Too many late nights in a row, too many excuses. Sure, our relationship had begun as an affair, but I told myself it was different.

He might've cheated on Jane, but he wouldn't do that to me. I was different. Our *love* was different. But the truth was simple. I didn't *want* to believe it. After all, why would someone who looked like *him* cheat on someone who looks like *me*?"

"*Can't fault her for modesty,*" Grim said.

"But a girl can only make so many excuses for her man," Tandy continued. "I didn't want to use my song against him, but it was my last resort. So I did. I started to use it whenever it was just the two of us. For a while, he didn't show any signs, and I felt relieved. I should have stopped there, but I didn't. The effects take time to show themselves full force, you know. So I kept it up. On the one hand, maybe I was just being jealous and insecure. Maybe there was no other woman. But on the other hand ... maybe there was.

"Then the signs started to show. He thought Jane was trying to shut down Medium Rare. I knew she didn't give a rat's tail about that, though. Deep down, Jane wanted nothing more than to never see or hear from Bruce again. And however much Jane wanted that, Ansel wanted it more.

"He's bought her a ring, you know," she said, and the mention of a proposal in the middle of what might turn into a confession threw me for a loop.

"I didn't know."

"Yes." She traced lazy circles around the lip of her cup with a delicate finger. "But he won't propose until he's certain she's moved on from Bruce for good. Well, I guess Ansel owes me one, now." She brought the tea to her lips, drinking deeply this time. "Bruce's paranoia got so bad that he brought me to Franco's Pizza for dates, thinking it would intimidate Jane into backing off, hoping it might save Medium Rare, which was never in danger of shutting down in the first place. Because let's be real, the town loves Tanner too much to see him lose the one place that feels like home to him."

But not too much to sit around doing nothing while he's wrongfully arrested, I thought bitterly.

"Anyway," she said with a wave of her hand, "Bruce's paranoia, coupled with the time I caught him talking to no one in bed one night when he thought I was asleep, made it obvious that my song had fallen on the ears of an impure soul."

"Can I ask you something?"

She smirked. "You just did."

Was she really being cute with me right now? Did she not realize how much trouble was about to come crashing down on her?

"Is it possible for a xana's song to backfire?"

"Huh?" Her nose crinkled along the bridge, making her look a little dim, a little ugly. And yeah, I took satisfaction from that. After all, she was a murderer, so I got to be petty, right?

"It's not making me paranoid," I said. "Your song. It still sounds like harp music to me. But what does it sound like to you? I can't imagine the soul of a murderer is exactly pure. Have you been paranoid lately, Tandy? Think you see things that aren't there? What if you made the whole thing up and it was actually *you* who became more paranoid each time you sang your song to Bruce until you were convinced he was cheating when he wasn't? What if you murdered him for no reason?"

Her gaze drifted listlessly around the room as she

considered it. "What? No. I couldn't have ... I know he was cheating on me. I didn't make a mistake. He deserved to die!" Her attention snapped to me. "You're trying to trick me, you lowly witch!"

Her beauty vanished in an instant.

She snarled as the harp played sharp and frantic. Her lengthy fingers gripped the handle of the iron kettle and she raised it up over her head. I was too slow to react. I tried to lift my arms to shield my face and deflect the blow that she aimed at me. Her strength and fury were terrifying, radiating off of her in blasts as she brought the kettle down on me and I closed my eyes and—

"Gaaaaah!" she screamed. When I opened them again, all I saw was a flash of black, like a shadow flying through the air.

Then it started to make sense.

Grim.

Deputy Manchester burst out of the bathroom and charged forward, and only after he had his cuffs out did Grim move from where he pinned Tandy to the floor, his massive jaws open around her neck.

As the deputy cuffed Tandy and pulled her roughly to her feet, Grim positioned himself between me and the murderer, plopping his big butt down, causing the floorboards to shudder under my feet as he did so.

Tandy resisted arrest as much as she could, but Deputy Manchester wasn't short on physical power. He easily managed her as she thrashed around, shouting like a psychopath, which she clearly was, that she would do everything in her power to get free and come back for me.

"Well, that's certainly not going to help your case in trial," Deputy Manchester said as he led her out the door.

Before he disappeared from sight, though, he told me, "Don't worry, Ms. Ashcroft. They always say these things once the cuffs go on. I lost count of how many death threats I had hovering over me, and yet here I am, surviving another day." He nodded once, decisively. "Good work, by the way."

As he walked her down the front steps, a wooden cart pulled up in front of the house. It looked like one that might have been attached to the back of a horse a hundred and some-odd years ago in Texas, but there was no horse. Just the cart. Hovering.

I mean, why not? If I was learning anything about magic, it was that questioning the how of it didn't lead anywhere. Best to just think, *Oh hey! That's neat!* and then get on with your day.

Or in this case, get on with your night.

I shut the door and turned to face the two remaining occupants. Grim was aggressively licking his balls by the fire, so I decided to focus my attention instead on Bruce, who, if I'd heard Ruby right earlier, wasn't long for this world.

The murder was solved. The murderer was arrested. Bruce had his closure.

Except he was still there. He hadn't disappeared.

Huh.

"Can I help you?" I asked but then realized how rude it sounded. That was no way to talk to a dead guy who was only now coming to terms with the fact that his girlfriend was the one that had done him in. "I just mean, I had hoped that would bring you the closure you needed to move on."

"I'd hoped so, too," he said, floating in the center of

the room, his arms folded over his chest, his face squinched up, though in pain or deep thought, I wasn't sure. Possibly both. After all, introspection too late in the game can be a form of slow torture. He focused his gaze on me, still wearing a pinched grimace as he said, "I've been a selfish jerk, haven't I?"

"Yes."

I know that's usually the point where you're supposed to lie and reassure the person that "anyone would've done that" or "it's not so bad in the scheme of things." But I couldn't bring myself to go there. This was Bruce's last opportunity for honesty. And I didn't get the impression he wanted me to simply make him feel better.

"I can sense it's almost time for me to go, but before I do," he said, "I need you to pass along a message for me."

"To?"

"Jane."

I nodded.

"Tell her that I realize now how selfish I've been— she'll appreciate that—but also let her know she was the only woman I truly loved, and I never deserved it in return."

Despite all the trouble his actions had caused, my heart ached for Bruce. But mostly it ached for Jane.

"She and Ansel are a much better fit. Let them know I send my blessing. And I know I've already asked enough of you, but if you could, explain to her that the especially hurtful things I did at the end—I wasn't myself. I don't say that for my sake, but for hers. I don't want her to think the man who married her, who knew her so intimately would deem her worthy of that especially cruel treatment under regular circumstances."

I understood. And I believed the request didn't come from a place of ego or self-preservation. "Of course," was all I managed to croak around the lump forming in my throat.

"Thank you, Nora."

And then Bruce Saxon slowly disappeared.

That was that, I supposed. It was finished. The murder was solved, and the spirit had moved on.

"Okay, fine." Grim's voice in my head made me jump. *"I give up. You win. Sleeping by the fire is way better than sleeping on that dusty porch in February."*

"Are you consenting to a bath?"

"Obviously."

"Good, because you smell like trash."

He smacked his big, floppy lips, sticking out his tongue. *"I taste like trash, too, if I'm totally honest."*

"Ew, I didn't need to know that."

"How about it? You ready to scrub me till all the ticks fall off?"

I sighed, bone tired. Had he not saved my life only a few minutes before, I would've said he could sleep outside one more night and we could deal with the bath in the morning.

But I supposed I owed him one ... if not my life.

"Yeah. Let's do this thing. Ruby said there's a hose out back."

I followed a few paces behind to avoid the brunt of his stink as we marched outside for a bonding experience neither of us was looking forward to.

Epilogue

❧

I slept like the dead and woke up the next morning to midday sunlight glowing from behind the thick curtains of Ruby's guest bedroom.

The questions that floated nebulously around my head as I fell asleep had crystallized overnight, and they bombarded me almost the moment I opened my eyes.

Now that the murder was solved, what was I supposed to do?

Should I try to get back to Texas?

Should I find a permanent place to live in Eastwind?

Would Ruby let me continue staying here for free?

What was my purpose in this town, now? How was I supposed to spend my free time?

Free time.

Now *there* was a foreign concept. I hated to admit how much the idea terrified me.

But then, in the space left by a whirlwind career and a string of unfulfilling relationships and, more recently, a murder to solve, new ideas began to populate. Exciting ones. Ones that had no point other than enjoyment.

I could go explore Eastwind.

I could visit Sheehan's Pub over in Erin Park.

Or see Rainbow Falls.

Or spend the day taste-testing at the farmer's market.

Or pop into one of the many clothing shops around the town centre (despite the magical cleanings, the same shirt and pants were overstaying their welcome; I'd stick with the coat, though, because I loved this coat).

Ooo! Or I could visit the animal sanctuary where Zoe worked.

Or I could find a magic shop and get some supplies. I possessed *some* level of magic, but I hadn't yet tested my limitations.

I was a witch.

I sat up in bed and laughed.

I was a witch!

As strange as it sounds, it hadn't set in until that moment. The hustle and bustle of adjusting to the strange new place and the pressure of finding who killed Bruce made it impossible for the reality to sink into my bones.

The day was bursting with exciting possibilities and none of them were, strictly speaking, productive.

Who *was* I, and what had happened to Nora Ashcroft?

Then the rest of the previous night settled in, and I remembered that I had one big, unpleasant to-do item to check off before I could get up to my whimsical shenanigans.

Having slept in so late, I'd missed Ruby's breakfast

time by a mile, and she was nowhere to be seen when I walked down, dressed for the day, and found Grim lying by the front door.

"*Son of a dog biscuit, I have to take a leak*," he said. "*I thought you might've died up there and I was going to have to empty the tank inside.*"

"You suddenly have a problem peeing indoors? Because that's not what your display in the sheriff's office led me to believe."

"*Exigent circumstances,*" he complained. "*You needed a diversion, and I provided. Don't hold it against me, or next time you need my help, all you'll get is a big, steaming pile of not-my-problem. Now can you open the door?*"

I didn't wait for him to finish before heading to Franco's Pizza. He caught up with me right as I turned onto the side street where the Italian restaurant was located.

Greta greeted me at the hostess stand.

"Just wanted to drop by to speak with Jane," I said.

"She's not working today."

"Really?" I asked, suddenly concerned. "Is everything okay?"

Greta looked at me like I'd lost my mind. "Yeah, everything's fine. It's just her day off."

"Oh. Right." *Some* people took days off. Noted. "Any chance you could tell me where she lives?"

I knew it was a long shot. I imagined someone walking into Chez Coeur and asking the hostess for my home address. If that wasn't the purpose of the security button under the host stand, I didn't know what was.

But this wasn't a big city. And despite the unusually

high murder rate, Eastwind wasn't the kind of place where everyone wandered around living in fear.

And I loved that.

Greta told me Jane's address without hesitation, and I thanked her and let Grim show me the way.

It was actually better that Jane was at home when I delivered Bruce's message.

I'll spare you the details, though. The summary is that Bruce's message was heard. There were tears (by both of us because I'm not a robot, okay?). Jane thanked me, and then I left her alone to presumably let the real waterworks begin.

She'd recover. She had Ansel.

And honestly, Bruce was kind of a terrible husband. And person. Sure, he came around in the end, but I wasn't sure if that made it all better. He still left broken women in his wake.

My feet led me to Medium Rare without my brain realizing where I was going.

But it made sense. It was where it all started for me in Eastwind.

And there was pie. Darn good pie.

I'm not ashamed to admit I do occasionally enjoy eating my feelings, and I had quite a few of them at the moment.

When Grim paused at the front doors, so did I. "What are you doing?"

"Waiting outside," he replied.

"But you smell so good. And you look like a completely different animal now."

"Exactly. I look like a walking black cotton ball. You didn't tell me a bath would make me frizz like this."

I rolled my eyes. *"I didn't know how your fur would react with magic. You look great. Just come in."*

"I doubt they want dogs inside."

"The place was run by a werewolf. Besides, Tanner wuvs you."

"You promised you wouldn't bring that up again," he said, growling.

I moved behind him and pushed him forward into the bustling late-lunch crowd at Medium Rare.

My suspicion was that as soon as Grim caught a whiff of steak, he'd stop putting up a fight. I was right.

Grim led the way over to an empty booth and made himself at home, climbing onto the seat and sitting up straight at the table. Okay then.

I'd heard that Bryant, one of the servers, had stepped up to manage the place while Tanner was in custody. I'd assumed that meant things would be a bit of a train wreck around here, but that didn't seem to be the case. None of the patrons appeared disgruntled, and most of the tables had plates of food in front of them already. Considering all the chaos around here, that was nothing short of a miracle. I hadn't met Bryant yet, but I already knew he deserved a raise.

And then the doors to the kitchen swung open and my breath caught in my chest.

Looked like Bryant didn't deserve the credit.

Tanner Culpepper hustled out of the kitchen with four plates stacked down his arms.

He must've gone straight from jail to Medium Rare or spent so little time at home that he didn't even bother shaving.

Ugh, his sandy brown facial hair was painfully

gorgeous. I suddenly imagined rubbing my face in it, really nestling in there. Then I imagined it was a blanket and I was rolling around in it and—

I glanced across the table at Grim.

I needed more non-dog friends, clearly.

"Nora!"

Even though I'd just been shamelessly ogling him, the suddenness of his voice caused me to jump. "Tanner! Hey! I didn't realize you were back."

"Liar," Grim said.

"Yeah," Tanner replied with an exhale, his eyes wide as he nodded his head slowly. "Just got out last night. Boy, am I glad to be out of there. I've *seen* some things, things that will haunt my dreams for— Oh! Hey, Grim!"

Tanner hopped over and was scratching Grim's sweet spot behind his ear before the hound could do a thing about it.

"Oh god, not in public," Grim whined as his paw thumped the plastic booth cushion again and again.

Tanner really got in there. "Who's a good boy?"

"I am! I'm a good boy!"

With a boop on Grim's nose, Tanner relented, and as my familiar swayed drunkenly, I ordered us each a steak and eggs.

Tanner brought out the food only a few minutes later, and as Grim shamelessly gorged himself on his plate, Tanner motioned for me to scoot over, which I did without hesitation. He slid in next to me, slinging his arm over the back of the booth, inspecting me closely. "What now, Nora?"

I shrugged. "I'm going to enjoy some steak and eggs."

"And then what? Try to get back to ... sorry, where are you from again?"

"Texas."

He chuckled. "Weird name, but okay. You gonna try to get back to Texas?"

I studied his face. "Nah. Not right away at least. I kind of like it here."

"It *is* a beautiful place."

"It's the people that make it for me, honestly," I said.

He flashed me a sneaky half-grin. "I could really use someone like you."

Do not faint! Do not faint!

"Oh yeah?" I asked coolly. "How would you use me?"

I mean, if we were crossing this line, why not cross it hard and fast, I say.

But his mind was *not* in the same place as mine.

"You have any experience waiting tables?"

I didn't mean to laugh right in his face, but it'd been a long couple days. I regained my composure before replying, "Yeah, I have a little experience waiting tables. Are you offering me a job, Mr. Culpepper?"

"Well," he said, leaning away from me and attempting a serious expression that looked about as natural on him as a pair of pants would on Grim, "it would be on a trial basis, of course. If you couldn't handle the pressure of working in Eastwind's top diner, then I'd have to let you go."

"I'll try not to let you down, sir," I said mockingly.

"Good. Then I'll see you tomorrow morning to start your training." He slid halfway out of the booth then paused, turning back toward me. "Oh, and one more thing."

"Yes?"

"Thanks for saving my hide." He leaned forward and before I realized what was happening, the kiss was already over. I refrained from touching the spot on my cheek where his lips had landed. "I owe you one," he said quietly, his face only inches from mine. "I mean it."

He hurried off as another customer waved him down.

"One what? He owes me one what?"

"I think it's pretty clear what he meant," Grim said. *"And let me say, if he does what you're thinking about even* half *as well as he scratches behind my ear, you're gonna want to call in that IOU immediately."*

"Oh, for fang's sake, Grim. Ulck. Please don't ever make that comparison again."

"Fine." He jabbed toward my plate with his big, frizzy paw. *"You gonna eat that? Because there's a good boy who would be happy to take it off your hands."*

"Don't even think about it. And stop drooling."

"I can't help that last part. Because if you didn't notice, I'm a dog."

"Yeah, yeah. You keep reminding me. Sounds like a cop-out, honestly."

Closing my eyes, I savored that first simple yet exquisite bite of yolk-covered steak, letting it all set in.

As fate had it, I'd died and found myself in Eastwind.

And when my innumerable acquaintances in Texas would inevitably gossip about my death and recite those empty words of, "She's in a better place now," I knew in my heart that those people would actually be correct.

End of Book 1

A Note from Nova

It's been a little over a year since I wrote this book and, sweet baby jackalope, what a year it's been!

I'm currently working on book 10 of the series, and I gotta tell you: I had NO idea how exciting Nora's story would become when I started writing *Crossing Over Easy*. None. As much as I'd like to brag, "Oh, I had it all planned out from the beginning..." Nope. I was totally clueless.

I was just getting to know Nora and Grim and Ruby and the rest, kind of like you are now. What I didn't realize was that they were also getting to know me... and learning how to manipulate my fingers into doing their bidding (especially Grim).

The next book in the series, *Death Metal*, gives Nora a little more time to settle into her new world, and then things really take off in book 3, *Third Knock the Charm*. The story gets its legs under it, and it's right about that time when readers start to yell at me for turning them into Eastwind addicts. Don't worry, I'm addicted, too. And so long as I have a single reader left, I'll keep writing about Eastwind because—fangs and claws!—it's fun.

I hope you'll stick around.

-Nova Nelson, 2/6/19

DEATH METAL
Eastwind Witches 2

As Nora Ashcroft settles into life in Eastwind and her job at Medium Rare, the spirit witch suspects she might have finally found a happy medium.

But when a wealthy werewolf is found dead and the police rule it a suicide, Nora's supernatural abilities might be the only thing that can uncover the truth surrounding the suspicious circumstances. Can she prove foul play?

Nora's mysteries continue in *Death Metal*

Grab your copy at
www.eastwindwitches.com/2

Get an exclusive Eastwind Witches book - free!

The Missing Motive follows a murder that takes place two years before Nora arrives in Eastwind.

With Sheriff Bloom by her side, Ruby True attempts to figure out who killed the insufferable druid who has taken up residence in her home.

Enjoy the divine duo of True and Bloom, and revisit some of your favorite Eastwind townsfolk in this humorous caper!

This book is only available to members of the Cozy Coven, Nova Nelson's reader group.

Go to www.cozycoven.com to join and claim your book!

You'll also receive updates from the town of Eastwind and gain access to games, quizzes, behind-the-scenes competitions, giveaways, and more!

About the Author

Nova Nelson grew up on a steady diet of Agatha Christie novels. She loves the mind candy of cozy mysteries and has been weaving paranormal tales since she first learned handwriting. Those two loves meet in her Eastwind Witches series, and it's about time, if she does say so herself.

When she's not busy writing, she enjoys long walks with her strong-willed dogs and eating breakfast for dinner.

Say hello:
nova@novanelson.com

Printed in Great Britain
by Amazon

11493903R00112